Grumpy Valentine

A Holiday Novella

DL White

Books by DL White

Copyright

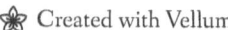

Author's Note

Dear Reader,

I'm gonna be real: this story was not supposed to go this way.

In January, I thought I might write a quick holiday short, a la my good, *good* girlfriend Danielle Allen's **Hot Holiday Hookups** (get into her, I love she). I was thinking maybe 20,000 words of fun and festive romance.

Well. Opal and Sterling had other plans and I went along with them. At nearly 40,000 words, Grumpy Valentine became a steamy, romantic, funny novella.

So here's the thing: this is a novella, which means it's shorter and more focused than my full-length romances. You'll get a complete story, but don't expect the deep character development of a novel. Think of it like a shot of top-shelf romance—concentrated, hot, and goes down smooth.

Content Warnings:

• Adult Sexual content- I don't include use of STI and birth control on the page. This should not be considered an indication of a forthcoming pregnancy

• Discussions of past relationship trauma - there is no physical or sexual violence in this novella

• Workplace professional themes- this is a workplace romance

Of all my characters, I think Sterling and Opal have the highest chance of returning, maybe in a fun extended epilogue that gives readers a peek into their future. I'm not really ready to let them go.

I so hope you'll enjoy exploring Opal and Sterling's world as much as I enjoyed creating them. The best stories happen when characters decide to write themselves!

Happy reading, and if you loved it, spread the good word! Please don't forget to review this title on your social media, at Goodreads or Storygraph.

XOXO,

DL White

Grumpy Valentine

The last thing tech developer Opal Richardson needs while launching a groundbreaking tech platform is a distraction. Especially not Sterling Carter, whose co-working space sits right across the courtyard from hers. He's sexy, charming..and keeps showing up with an uncanny ability to climb right over her carefully constructed walls.

Sterling Carter's recent return to Atlanta was supposed to be about launching his PR firm, not falling for the tall, stunning, sharp-tongued woman who challenges him from day one. Despite their instant chemistry, Opal's painful past makes her hesitant to mix business with pleasure.

When a severe storm traps them together, their connection becomes impossible to ignore, sparking a passionate encounter that could either heal her wounds or break her heart completely.

Set in Atlanta's bustling tech scene, GRUMPY VALENTINE is a steamy workplace romance where love moves at startup speed.

Grumpy Valentine

Chapter One

S terling

My first mistake on day one in my new office building was thinking I could wing it at a shop called *Coffee Theory*. After years of no-nonsense New York coffee runs, I should have known my first morning back in Atlanta would hit different.

I'd walked into the bright ground-floor space just as sunrise was starting to stream through the floor-to-ceiling windows, hoping to grab a quick coffee before heading up to my temporary office. Instead, I found myself squinting at an elaborate menu board while the morning crowd shuffled impatiently behind me.

"Sir," the barista said for the third time, "what size would you like? We offer precise, proper, or plentiful."

"Uh... medium? Which is that?"

"That would be proper."

"So your small is called precise and medium is proper? And large is...plentiful? Do I have that right?"

My barista—Joya, according to her name tag—wore her locs in an impressive updo dotted with copper beads that matched the café's fixtures. Her layered necklaces were made of the same beaded material and made pleasant sounds as she gestured to the menu board, where elaborate botanical illustrations described each drink.

"The theory here," she explained, "is that coffee consumption should be intentional—exactly what you need and no more. Each size is calibrated for the optimal ratio of espresso to milk to flavoring. Precise is perfect for a straight shot or a concentrated flavor experience. Proper balances all elements evenly, and plentiful gives you more of the complementary ingredients without overwhelming the flavor of the brew itself."

"Uh huh. The...brew?"

She smiled. "The brew, served in varying strengths and flavor profiles. The house blend is a medium roast with notes of dark chocolate and blackberry. I personally think the Ethiopian single-origin is the way to go if you drink it black."

"Okay, and..." I smirked. "Why is that?"

"Well, the flavor profile is complex—"

"Joya!" A sharp voice cut through our coffee education moment. "Come on! I have things to do."

I turned to address the woman having a tantrum behind me and...*dayum.*

She was striking—smooth, deep brown skin with elegant angles to her face and full lips thinned into an impatient line. Everything about her was exacting, from the twist-out falling past her shoulders to the thick, dark-rimmed glasses perched on her nose. The tailored blazer and pencil skirt she wore emphasized her curves in all the right places.

"Maybe you can practice your pick-up lines after the morning rush," she said, stepping up to the counter. "The rest of us would like to order coffee so we can get to work."

I laughed, which appeared to piss her off more. Raising both hands in apology, I attempted to smooth things over. My first day in the building was not going well.

"I uh...I was actually just trying to get the lay of the land so I could order coffee. Good job going hard for the helpless barista forced to answer my questions about the coffee she serves, though."

Her jaw tightened and I caught a flash behind her eyes just before it dissipated. She shifted her weight, designer laptop bag sliding against her hip. The movement drew my eye to the point where her waist narrowed, creating a sexy cola bottle shape. She was definitely a sight for sore eyes.

I guess I'd been staring a beat too long. She sent me a glare that I read as eyes up here, asshole.

"Either you're new here," she said, meting out her words slowly, "or new to ordering coffee at a cafe in the morning, but this is a busy time of day. If you wouldn't mind stepping aside, we'd all be most grateful. You can pick up the flirting right where you left off."

I forced myself to turn back to Joya before I got into real trouble. "Let me try that Ethiopian blend you suggested. Proper, since..." I glanced back at the most beautiful dark brown eyes I'd seen in a long time. "I'm holding up the line. Also, my apologies if I was offensive."

I tapped my credit card at the mobile pay station, then stepped aside to wait for my drink. Joya was already reaching for a cup as the woman stepped to the counter.

"The usual, Opal?"

"Please. And I'm sorry about—" She glanced my way, lowering her voice, but I caught the gesture at me and Joya's laugh in response.

"You're always ruining my fun. I was having a good time."

"I know how you like to nerd out over coffee. You would have held us all hostage while you explained every detail of the menu."

She ended up waiting for her drink a few feet away from me, head bowed over her phone in her hand. The urge to poke at her was too strong to resist.

"So...what's your usual?" I asked, making it obvious I was speaking to her. "She asked if you wanted your usual. You're clearly a regular and I'm still learning."

Her fingers paused on her screen for just a second. I watched her debate whether to ignore me entirely, but in the end, she bit out a quick reply. "Precise americano, extra hot, half a pump of hazelnut and a splash of half-and-half."

"Ah. Kind of takes longer to order it than to make it. If it's your usual, it must hit like nirvana."

That got me a flicker of attention, even if she didn't look up from her phone. "It's efficient."

"Efficient," I repeated, testing the word. "You speak like a person who has their whole day planned down to the minute."

Now she did look at me, which I counted as a win even if her expression suggested I was being graded and coming up short. There was something in her eyes, though. A glint she couldn't quite hide behind the cool assessment.

"Are you always this chatty with strangers?"

"Actually, yes. Especially when I'm learning the local customs. Like not flirting with baristas, apparently. I'm usually smoother than that."

Her lips twitched. Almost a smile. Almost. "Everything's custom here, but Joya's a pro, so you need to know what you want, order it, then step aside."

"Hmm. I should probably take notes, then since I'll be in here often. What other Coffee Theory etiquette should I know about?"

"Here you go, Opal," Joya called out, setting a cup on the counter. "I'll have yours right up, sir. It's brewing."

She stepped forward to claim her coffee, then paused. "Don't hold up the line with twenty questions. Get that rule down first."

I watched her head for the door, appreciating how the fit of her skirt was perfect for her stride. The whole package was something else—beautiful, sharp tongued...and clearly used to keeping people at a distance.

That kind of woman made a man want to work for her attention.

"Proper Ethiopian," Joya said, sliding my cup across the counter. "I didn't catch your name, but I did hear you tell Opal you'll be here often."

"Sterling," I said, picking up my order. "I'm moving in on thirty-two, but it's under renovation, so they've got me in a co-working space in the interim. You will definitely be seeing me."

Joya beamed a welcoming smile. "Well, welcome to The Avian. The community is pretty great here. I look forward to learning your usual order. Oh, and don't mind Opal. You have to get to know her."

I sipped my coffee, pausing to give Joya an appreciative eyebrow raise at the smooth, rich flavor, and used the other hand to sling my laptop bag over my shoulder.

"Noted. Something tells me getting to know Opal is the trick."

The Avian was one of those Atlanta high-rise buildings that tried to have it all—old money prestige with new money amenities. The corporate offices that leased permanent space took up the top floors while the bottom floors were leased as co-working spaces to attract the city's growing freelance crowd. Coffee Theory occupied prime real estate on the ground floor, the copper fixtures and upholstered leather chairs striking a balance between luxury and approachability.

My brother, Sedrick, had stumbled onto The Avian while scouting temporary office space for me in the months before I relocated to Atlanta. He had a knack for spotting hidden opportunities and had never steered me wrong.

I flashed my keycard and stepped onto the elevator, then got off on twenty-three. Half of the floor was dedicated to open workspace ranging from hot desks to dedicated pods. The other half housed private offices and conference rooms. My workspace was an impersonal monthly rental—not quite the corner suite waiting for me on thirty-two once renovations finished, but it was comfortable enough for now.

The building formed a U-shape, giving me a clear view across an attractive courtyard. Movement drew my eye, and I saw her.

Opal, settling into a chair and pulling up to a desk.

I'd barely settled in myself when my phone buzzed in my pocket. I dug it out, swiping Sedrick's name and professional Realtor headshot away with my thumb.

"I hope I'm interrupting your beauty sleep," he said, by way of greeting. "Can't be better looking than me."

"Funny. I'm already at the office." I took another sip of coffee. "The shop in this building is uh...quirky is a good word for it. The coffee's good, though."

"Yeah, they take themselves pretty seriously." I heard the shuffling of papers in the background. "First, I just checked the voicemail and we got a message from the contractor working on your office. They're saying another three weeks on the build-out."

"Three weeks?" I leaned back in my chair, watching Opal pace the length of the window with her phone plastered to her ear. "What happened to two?"

"Supply chain issues, apparently. What are ya gonna do?" Sedrick had handled all the real estate arrangements when I decided to relocate from New York to Atlanta. I had more money than time, and Sedrick understood the assignment. "On the bright side," he added, "I might have found you a condo. It's a newer build in Midtown, walking distance to the office. Way better than that corporate apartment you're in."

"The apartment is fine."

"The apartment is temporary. I'm trying to get you into something that'll tie you to Atlanta. It's time to start putting down some roots, little brother."

"I just got here."

"Ma is already sending me all the houses for sale around the neighborhood. You know, in case you want to go ahead and buy a house."

"I don't know if I'm in for a four-bedroom home in Stone Mountain, Georgia, minutes from my mother. The traffic will make me want to do unspeakable things. At the same time, I'm not looking for a slick, new place in Midtown. The rent in-town is ridiculous. I need something nice, affordable, not downtown. I don't mind driving, but I don't want to be on the road all morning. Can you expand your search to those parameters?"

He sighed. I felt his eyes rolling. "Fine. Just know Pop is

all about Sunday dinners. You don't want to be too far from the folks. He's not gonna hear nothing about how far you are from them."

I smiled despite myself. Moving back to Atlanta hadn't been my original plan, but the shakeup at my former firm had shifted things. Lower cost of living, built-in network, family nearby—it made sense to base my new consulting firm in my hometown instead of trying to compete in the New York market.

"Let's grab dinner tonight," Sedrick suggested. " I can show you the specs for this condo you're turning down. I bet I can talk you into it."

"I told you what I'm looking for, Sedrick. What you need to show me is condos in my price range in the area I want to live in."

"I heard you, bro. Don't make me pull rank. I'm still the oldest."

"And the shortest with the least amount of hair and even less muscle tone. Have you ever heard of a gym?"

"See, what you're not gonna do is insult my trainer. Just wait till I see you. Cypress Street at seven? You can walk there from your place."

"Make it six. I'm not trying to hang out all night like a fifty-year-old man who thinks he's still twenty-one."

I hung up on his laugh, then fired up my laptop to tackle the mountain of emails that came with starting your own consulting firm. I already had a few contracts to finalize and invoices to email out. My assistant had just put in her notice at her current employer and wouldn't be starting for a few weeks, so I was on my own. I already couldn't wait for her to start.

The desk line, which I had just discovered was plugged in and working, warbled on the corner of my desk.

Chapter Two

pal

Coffee Theory was my daily salvation.

After escaping ConnecTech's idea of a *collaborative environment*— namely a workplace where a closed door was mere suggestion and there was always a team-building exercise happening in the common areas, The Avian's mix of private offices and co-working spaces was the closest thing to heaven. The real draw was Coffee Theory, the building's ground floor café that served brewed coffee offered with minimal small talk, and a barista who knew exactly how I liked my americano.

Even on my worst days at The Avian, at least I could count on starting my morning right.

Or I usually could.

Joya, the owner and morning Barista at Coffee Theory

was explaining the entire concept of the business to some guy holding up the line. "The house blend is a medium roast with notes of dark chocolate and blackberry. I personally think the Ethiopian single-origin is the way to go if you drink it black."

"Okay. And...why is that?"

I shifted my weight, checking my watch. This man was really about to turn my morning coffee run into a full seminar.

"Well, the flavor profile is complex—"

"Joya!" I called out, angling around him. The sparkle in her eye told me she was enjoying this little coffee education session. Traitor. "Come on, I have things to do!"

He turned to see who was interrupting his private tasting. I felt his eyes take me in from my deep purple ribbed top and matching jacket to my pencil skirt, styled twist-out and thick-rimmed glasses. I was taller than a lot of women, so I was used to commanding attention, but the way he slowly dragged his eyes down, then back up my body made my skin tingle.

Not that I was paying attention.

"Maybe you can practice your pick-up lines after the morning rush," I said, stepping up to the counter. "The rest of us would like to order coffee so we can get to work."

He laughed—*actually* laughed, which only irritated me more. Then he had the nerve to raise both hands in mock surrender, like I was the one being unreasonable.

"I uh...I was actually just trying to get the lay of the land so I could order coffee," he said, still smiling. "Good job going hard for the helpless barista forced to answer my questions about the coffee she serves, though."

I leveled him with a look that I hoped said exactly what I thought about his charm offensive. "Either you're new here, or new to ordering coffee at a cafe *in the morning,* but this is a busy time of day. If you wouldn't mind stepping aside, we'd all be most grateful. You can pick up the flirting right where you left off."

When he finally stepped aside, I approached the counter with relief.

"Morning, Opal. Your usual?" Joya asked.

"Yes, please. And I'm sorry about—" I lowered my voice, gesturing his way.

Joya laughed. "You're always ruining my fun. I was having a good time."

"I know how you like to nerd out over coffee. You would have held us all hostage while you explained every detail of the menu." I tapped the glass window on the display case, pointing at the tray of freshly baked, buttery croissants. "And add one of those. With my schedule, I will not resist bread today."

"You've been here really early lately. I bet you're here late, too." Joya glanced over her shoulder, speaking up to be heard over the milk steamer.

"Yeah, I've been pulling some long days. My department is swamped with our upcoming platform launch. You wouldn't know it, though. All everyone wants to talk about is this gala next weekend. It'll be a good time but I have bigger priorities."

"Well, don't burn yourself out," she chided gently. "You know The Man don't care a single thing about your health. They'll replace you the very next day. I want to keep seeing you around here."

"I know you're not talking, Joya. You are here every morning at what time? Four AM? I am not that dedicated to any job." I swiped my phone across the credit card reader to pay for my order. "I'll be fine so long as that croissant keeps me from biting someone's head off."

"Breakfast of champions," Joya said. "Oh, and it's the second Tuesday of the month. We have our service industry community meeting so I'm closing up early today. Make sure you get down here for lunch."

"Yes, Mom."

"Get an attitude if you want," said Joya. "You'll try to make coffee and a croissant last you all day knowing it don't work like that."

I moved a few feet away to wait for my drink, scrolling through my inbox which was already overflowing with morning requests.

"So... what's your usual?"

I glanced up to find him leaning in, making it obvious he was speaking to me. "She asked if you wanted your usual. You're clearly a regular and I'm still learning."

My fingers paused on the screen. Part of me wanted to ignore him entirely, but I also realized I was hangry and under-caffeinated. I bit out a quick reply. "Precise americano, extra hot, half pump of hazelnut and a splash of half-and-half."

"Ah." He nodded deeply, like he knew me better by knowing my coffee order. "Kind of takes longer to order it than to make it. If it's your usual, it must hit like coffee nirvana."

I hit him with a look that said he was dancing too close to my last nerve. "Are you always this chatty with strangers?"

"Actually, yes. Especially when I'm learning the local customs," he said. "Like not flirting with baristas, apparently. I'm usually smoother than that."

My lips twitched. I had no doubt this man thought he

was being smooth. "Everything's custom here, but Joya's a pro, so you need to know what you want, order it, then step aside."

"Hmm. I should probably take notes since I'll be in here often," he said. "What other coffee shop etiquette should I know about?"

"Here you go, Opal," Joya called out, setting my order on the counter. "I'll have yours right up, sir. It's brewing."

I stepped forward to claim my coffee and croissant, then paused, turning to toss one last barb over my shoulder. "Don't hold up the line with twenty questions. Get that rule down first."

As I headed for the door, I was very aware of his eyes following me. And even more aware that part of me didn't mind.

With my latte in one hand and the croissant tucked into a paper bag, I wound through the maze of tables and couches to the lobby and grabbed an elevator. The ride to fifteen was blissfully empty. The other tenants on the floor seemed to understand the meaning of personal space. There were no pop-ins for casual chat, no loud conversations by the water cooler. Even the cleaning crew had learned to work around my hours.

I unlocked my office and walked through a small seating area that I called the lounge. My office was just big enough for the desk and my chair, so I used the lounge for the rare meetings I held at Avian and for a change of scenery if needed.

All three of my monitors flickered on as I settled at my desk and plugged my laptop into the dock. I began my day as I usually did, by pulling up the latest analytics on ConnecTech's diversity initiatives project.

The Align Hiring Platform was practically my life's

work. Diversity and Inclusion weren't buzzwords and policy to me; they were my passion. Throughout undergrad and grad school programs, I was acutely aware of how people were treated differently based on race, gender, class, and aspects of identity. It felt so fundamentally wrong, so when I stumbled onto a career path that allowed me to drive measurable, systemic change, I jumped at the opportunity.

Now my bread and butter was programming a hiring and onboarding platform for employers that would make a tangible difference in the lives of underrepresented professionals across dozens of industries. Beta testing was showing promising results, but we needed stronger engagement metrics before the full launch.

I paused my deep dive into data and user trends to lead two meetings and get a status update from my staff. By the time I ended the Teams call, my eyes were dry and I felt a headache coming on.

A glance at the clock showed it was nearly noon. Time always flew when I was debugging other people's mistakes, though I wouldn't exactly call it fun. Between the platform launch and the upcoming Circuit2Soul gala that everyone at ConnecTech wouldn't stop talking about, my to-do list kept multiplying. Yes, it would be a great networking opportunity. Yes, I was excited to demo our flagship platform. But the thought of playing nice with potential investors and clients made my anxiety spike.

My phone lit up with my best friend's face. Her high cheekbones and mega-watt smile took up the whole screen. I briefly considered letting it go to voicemail, but Asia had a sixth sense—with accompanying attitude—about avoiding her calls.

"Hey. I'm in a zone."

"I'll be quick!" Asia's voice hit a pitch that made me

cringe. Not because it was annoying, but because it usually meant trouble. "What color is your dress for the gala? I just picked up mine and realized we never coordinated."

I eyed the garment bag hanging on my office door. "This could have been a text, Asia. Black Tadashi."

"You don't answer texts," she replied with a deep sigh. "And of course, you're going with a plain black dress."

"It is not plain. The top is a V-neck, the skirt is a long, kinda flowy black maxi thing. It's elegant with some drama. Just hush, you'll like it."

"Are you sure you don't want something with a little more color? Let's go shopping tomorrow."

"Can't." I tapped through my calendar, confirming what I already knew. "I have meetings on meetings. I'm running out of time to work out these issues with the platform."

"They can't have one meeting without you?"

"Oh, yes," I answered quickly. "Yes, they can. And when I come back, everything will be assigned to me because no one else knows how to answer questions or resolve issues. Also, all the decisions they do make on their own will be wrong. I need to be in every meeting right now. Sorry, Boo."

I tried to look sad. It did not work. "But we both know you're going to shop anyway. FaceTime me, so you can show me all the dresses I wouldn't dare allow to touch these ass cheeks."

"Actually, it's okay, because I found this sparkly silver and white backless number and I didn't want to clash with whatever you chose."

"Now you know good and well—"

"You never know! You might get a wild hair up your ass one time and show up in red." She shifted into a tone that meant she was up to something. "Speaking of surprises...Jordan invited his frat brother Elliott to the gala. He is very single, very successful, and—"

"I'm very much not interested in being set up at a work event, Asia. I'd be a boring date."

"You would not—"

A loud chime from my laptop cut her off. I tabbed over to my email, scanning the latest message from the marketing team. The curse that slipped out was entirely involuntary.

"I heard that. What happened?"

I sighed, letting my eyelids close briefly. "Remember I told you our head of marketing was leaving ConnecTech? We thought he was going to give like four weeks' notice so we could get past the gala and the launch?"

"Right. It'd be a nightmare if he left all of that to someone else."

"Well, guess who he left the nightmare to?"

"What?" She screeched so loud I pulled the phone from my ear. "How did you get in it? You don't even work in marketing."

"Well, somebody got petty with him about leaving, so he made it a four-hour notice and bounced. And somehow, because I have a marketing background, all the questions and tasks are falling into my lap. I'm trying to finalize our sneak peek of the Align platform at the gala and I'm working on the official launch...and now I'm apparently the acting VP of marketing?"

"Oh, honey. No wonder you don't have time to shop. What does Scott say about all of that?"

I pushed out a grunt. Scott was nice, but he was a pushover—a trait I'd used to my advantage. When I almost quit because I couldn't handle working at home with my neighbor's TV blaring and children running and screaming at all hours, but I also couldn't work at the loud, distracting office, he worked out a deal to rent a co-working space and let me work at The Avian.

"Who do you think is sending the emails suggesting I might be able to help?"

"Oh for fuck's sake, Opal."

"Trust, we are going to have a heart-to-heart very soon, because..." I inhaled, then exhaled, then repeated the practice until my heartbeat slowed to normal sinus rhythm. "We need to change the subject before I have a stroke. What else is up?"

"Actually...I have a question." Asia practically squealed, which almost set my teeth on edge. "Well, less of a question and more of a demand."

"This does not bode well."

"I was hoping you didn't have plans for Friday night and could join Jordan and me at Marcel for dinner."

I'd only been to the elegant, first-rate steak restaurant once, and for very good reason. "You want me to spend my whole paycheck on a steak? On Valentine's Day?"

"It would be our treat, of course. We booked ages ago. We only go there when it's a super special occasion—"

"Their ribeye steak is over a hundred dollars, Asia. It better be a super special occasion."

"We've been talking about getting married for a year, and yesterday he told me that he switched our reservation to a bigger table. I think he's going to pop the question! You have to come!"

The laugh I barked out scared us both. "Girl, I know you don't expect me to third-wheel on your proposal date."

Asia sucked her teeth. "No, Opal. I expect you to find someone to bring with you! I'm saving two seats. You and...someone of your choice. Unless you want me to invite Elliott?"

"I am not amused."

"Opal, when was the last time you went on a date?"

"When was the last time you called just to chat instead of trying to fix me up?"

"Yesterday, when you didn't answer my call. And this morning, when you also didn't answer my call."

"I didn't even see that you called. You're always doing this to me. I have a ton of shit to do and I could use the quiet time to work. Have someone record the proposal and send it to me."

"Opal Simone!" She whined, putting on that pouty expression she'd perfected. "Do not even pretend you're trying to miss this dinner. I will not let you hide behind work forever."

"I'm not hiding. I'm a busy executive who is strategic about her time."

"Mmhmm." She looked like she didn't believe me. Hell, I didn't believe me either. "I've gotta go. Meeting in ten. We'll talk about it later. Can you do lunch tomorrow if I bring it to you, and I don't sit down? I can just stand in the doorway and scarf down a salad."

I half snorted, half laughed. Her smart-ass commentary was disarming and always why I couldn't fight with her. "Fine. Meet me at Coffee Theory. I reserve the right to text you if I need to cancel."

She giggled. "Pencil me in your hellish calendar for about one o'clock."

I hung up and went back to the stack of tasks I needed to complete before code review. I couldn't showcase a new platform with obvious flaws and janky workflow, not to mention tired stock images and uninspired copy. I was immediately lost in test user feedback, grateful for the silence that let me actually think.

* * *

My stomach reminded me I'd worked straight through lunch. Again.

I grabbed my phone and rushed down to Coffee Theory, only to find the steel gates already pulled down and the cafe dark.

"Damn it!" I hissed, throwing a mini-tantrum in the hallway. "She even reminded me."

"Great minds," said a smooth, deep voice behind me.

I turned to find Mr. Twenty Questions, the man who had been holding up the coffee line, standing there with an apologetic smile.

"I'm about to head over to Metro Diner," he said, referencing a well-known eatery a block away. "I hear they do a great Philly cheese. I'll be the judge of that. Care to join me? It'll make up for annoying you this morning."

I stared at him, briefly considering his offer and fully ignoring the fluttering in my belly. I'd managed to miss the tastefully sized diamond winking in his left ear, and how his charcoal gray sport coat stretched nicely across his broad shoulders. A neatly groomed goatee framed a smile that probably got him out of trouble on a regular basis. Nuns were probably wooed by warm brown eyes, smooth skin, and chiseled cheekbones.

His brand of handsome made women forget schedules, commitments...marriage vows. All of those features on one man were too tempting a combination for me.

"I worked through lunch and I was just hoping to get something to take the edge off, but...." I stepped back toward the elevator bank. "Thanks. I'll hit the vending machine."

His smile didn't falter. "Rain check, then."

Back in my office, I inhaled a bag of chips, some chocolate candies and guzzled a swig of cola, but it wasn't doing anything for me. I was hungry and frustrated.

And distracted.

Who was that guy, anyway? Why was I seeing him so much—twice on one day in a busy high-rise office building?

I hoped he was not planning to make a pest of himself. Though...he would hardly be classified as a pest. At least he seemed nice. He took my terse direction that morning better than he should have. He was probably the kind of man who remembered his assistant's birthday and brought coffee and donuts for the office just because it was Friday.

"Meh," I grumbled to myself. "No thanks to a chummy, talky...*fine as hell* nice guy."

The cursor blinked in steady rhythm while my mind wandered. Did his voice always have that deep timbre that dragged across the nerve endings on my back and made parts of my body thump?

Were his well-veined hands as strong when they gripped a set of wide hips as they'd seemed this morning as he fiddled with the cafe business card he'd plucked from the holder on the counter?

I sat up, waving a hand as if I could push the thoughts away. "Get it together," I whispered aloud to no one. There was no reason to be imagining how that goatee would feel against the sensitive, tender skin of my inner—

Five strong knocks boomed at my office door, making me nearly jump out of my skin. I stood, pulling at my jacket and crossed the room. Through the frosted glass panel alongside the wood door frame, a familiar broad-shouldered silhouette appeared.

My heart did a traitorous little skip as I pulled the door open. "You always bang on a door like you're five-oh?"

That smile was back, bending those thick lips as he

stood there holding a paper bag from Metro Diner. The scent that came off that bag made my mouth water.

"I apologize. I'm Sterling, by the way. I realized I never introduced myself. Anyway, the chicken Philly and fries was the special today. I got two and I brought you one."

I stared at him, almost not believing what I was seeing. He...brought me lunch? "Opal...and how—I'm not in the directory. How did you know where..."

"Don't think me weird, but I realized I can see your office from mine on twenty-three." He stepped inside far enough to set the bag on the low table in front of a two-seater couch, sending waves of a musky mix of leather and vanilla scent in his wake.

He glanced at my desk, probably noting the can of cola and empty wrappers flanking my keyboard, then brought his eyes back to mine. "The thought of you making do with a paltry vending machine lunch while my belly was full disturbed me."

"Uhm...thanks. What do I owe you?"

He smiled. "I owed you. Enjoy your lunch."

Before I could form a coherent response, he was pulling the door shut behind him. My stomach growled in betrayal as I grabbed the brown paper bag. Inside, I found a stack of extra napkins, salt, pepper and ketchup tucked alongside the sandwich wrapped in foil and a container of crispy fries.

Of course he was thoughtful.

I rushed to the window, scanning the offices across the courtyard. After a few moments, I noticed movements a few floors above mine. He stood in the window, hands in his pockets. Then he waved and stepped back.

Well. Wasn't he...nice?

It would be just my luck that he would feel welcome to visit entirely too often, bringing the distraction of that smile and well-cut suit and delicious cologne. He might make me hope and dream about liking a man. Falling for a man.

Letting a man convince me to identify as a crab leg because I could deal with getting all the way cracked open.

I didn't have time for any of that.

Damn if I was going to turn down a free lunch, though.

Chapter Three

S terling

Atlanta shouldn't be this cold.

I'd expected a break from New York winters, but this year the city had other plans. The bitter wind cutting through my wool coat and cashmere scarf felt more like Manhattan than Georgia. Pushing through the heavy wooden door of Cypress Street Pub felt like coming in from a storm.

Some things never changed. The exposed brick walls still wore decades of stories like badges of honor. The hardwood floors still groaned in familiar places. They'd updated the art on the walls and reupholstered the booths, but the soul of the place remained unchanged—young professionals at the bar loosening their ties, Georgia State students circled around the pool tables, old-timers who'd been coming here since before I was born holding court in their usual spots.

Sedrick had already claimed our table—the same one where we used to plot his first real estate deal over cheap pitchers of beer. These days my big brother was nursing what looked like club soda with lime instead of his usual Jack and Coke.

"Don't tell me you're turning over a new leaf." I slid into my seat, nodding at his decidedly light drink choice. "What happened to the guy who used to go shot for shot with me at Five Paces?"

"That guy turned fifty and found out one drink hits like a whole pint now. Three-day hangovers ain't the move." He pushed a menu my way, pure habit since we both knew it by heart. "Plus my trainer would have words. Some of us actually have to work for this body."

"A trainer?" I poked his meaty shoulder, remembering how he used to bench press me when we were younger. "You're almost up to a whole pushup, right?"

"Keep talking. I was at the house last week. Mom's going through old photos for Kindred Art Gallery's social media. Wouldn't take much to get her to post those baby pictures she's been hoarding. I got some caption ideas already."

"You wouldn't dare."

"Try me." His grin was pure mischief as he flagged down Savannah, who'd been serving us since our college days. She'd watched us grow from rowdy twenty-somethings into the professionals we pretended to be now. "You know what you want? I'm starving."

We ordered wings for me, some Mediterranean plate with grilled chicken for Sedrick, and before Savannah could even walk away, my brother had his tablet out and loaded up. The realtor never slept.

"I know, I know," he started, hands raised in preemptive

defense. "Just look at the listing." He turned the screen to show me a two-story Craftsman, all gray siding and stone accents and a manicured lawn. "Three bedrooms on Highland Ave in Morningside. Prime location, close to Piedmont Park, two-car garage, home office space—"

"Does the house come with a family?" I took a pull from my beer, some local IPA that would've been too fancy for this place back in the day. "What am I gonna do with three bedrooms and an office? I have one car, and those photos are making my wallet cry. That mortgage is going to be too rich for my blood."

"Use the other half of the garage for a gym."

"This is how I know you have no idea how much space gym equipment takes up."

The wadded napkin he threw caught me between the eyes. "Would you shut your mouth and open your ears? Why not invest in something permanent before the market turns? Put down some real roots. It won't be just you forever."

"My money is building my business." I picked up his napkin projectile and threw it back with better aim. After a year of corporate downsizing had eliminated my position as President of PR Strategy, the severance package had given me a chance to build something of my own. "You took a year to buy your first place because you wanted the perfect property."

"I was being strategic."

"And what do you think I'm doing? You're just trying to get me settled like you. Is it lonely out there in suburbia?"

"Don't knock it. My bed stays warm and occupied, and that stove lights up every night."

"I appreciate you wanting me to have what you think is the good life. My future might not even be in Atlanta. I've got clients everywhere now—LA, New York, Chicago, international—"

"You can't serve them from a home base where you've put down roots?" Sedrick leaned forward, his eyes aglow. "Don't let Pop hear a hint of you talking about not getting where you need to go. He'll go off about how he helped make Hartsfield one of the busiest airports in the world. You could be anywhere in hours."

Our food arriving saved me from the same argument we'd been having for the past year. We fell into the comfortable silence of brothers who didn't need to fill every moment with talk. Some things hadn't changed since the days we plotted his first deals over cheap beer.

Sedrick made light work of his meal and pushed his plate away, wiping his hands. "Hey, you got a tux? You should come to this thing with Blair and me next weekend. The guest list is the who's who of Atlanta tech. Every major company sends people to schmooze. It would be a perfect networking opportunity, especially since you're just getting back to the city. A lot has changed, man."

I wiped wing sauce from my fingers. "Who's throwing it?"

"The Diversity in Tech Coalition. It's a big formal thing —black tie, silent auction, champagne, the works." He pulled up another tab on his tablet. "My firm's handling property deals for some of the company CEOs, so I scored extra tickets. Bring somebody. Make it a proper double date."

"Right, because what I want to do with my Saturday night is drag a random woman around while I'm trying to network."

Laughter erupted from the next table. I caught Sedrick's

knowing smirk. The place was filling up, the after-work crowd giving way to people out for the evening.

"So where's Blair tonight?"

"Shaw's basketball team has a pre-playoffs meeting tonight, so Blair's picking him up." He stole one of my wings, ignoring my glare as he stripped it clean. "Seriously though, come to the gala. These tech companies love throwing money at consultants. It'll be like shopping for clients. Your kind of crowd."

I watched him check his phone, probably another text from Blair. A familiar twinge twisted my gut. Sed had a perfect life—a successful career, a beautiful wife balancing her law practice with team mom duties, a son already taller than both of us at fifteen and destined for a sports scholarship at a school of his choice.

Meanwhile, I was starting over. Temporary apartment. Coworking office space.

Wings for dinner.

I didn't feel behind, just...on a different path, one I'd chosen. The severance package and my parents' lessons in saving had given me a chance to build something meaningful, something entirely mine. Even being back in Atlanta felt right, like those New York years had been preparation for appreciating the rhythm of home.

"My kind of crowd meaning..." I snatched the last wing before he could think about it, waving it at him.

He sneered, his lip curling, before returning to his pitch. "Meaning they're serious about real change, not just checking boxes. The Coalition does panel discussions, tech demos, awards ceremonies. They're about making moves, not repeating buzzwords. The after-party's supposed to be fire too. They had some Grammy winner perform last year."

I chewed my chicken wing and pondered. It did sound

like exactly what I needed to get involved in. These companies all had initiatives, but how many were making real impact? How were those efforts landing in the community?

That's where I could make a difference.

"Alright, I'm in. But no date. I'm there to work."

"You're always there to work." Sedrick reached for his wallet, glancing at his phone again. Blair was probably hitting him up back to back. "One of these days you'll admit you moved home for more than business. Maybe find your own Blair, get a nice house, give Shaw some cousins..."

"Man, you're soft as shit. Remember when you swore you was gonna be a player? Mr. Loverboy. Now you're glued to that phone and I know it's your wife. Probably talking about how naked she's gonna be when you get home."

"I wish." He sucked his teeth. "She's talking about hitting Kroger on my way home for raspberry chocolate ice cream 'cause it's on sale." The head shake was all for show. We both knew Blair could ask for the moon and he'd try to get up there and grab it. "Don't get shit twisted. I can still take you."

"Says the man eating fake rice. How you gonna fight me with no fuel?"

"It's quinoa, you uncultured swine." His phone alerted again. "Now Shaw wants nuggets. When did I become UberEats?"

"Tell him Uncle Sterling says champions don't eat fast food." Pride swelled in my chest. That kid was going places, and not just because of his jump shot. He had Sedrick's strategy mind and Blair's drive, plus a talent all his own.

"I'm out. Orders coming in mean people getting snippy if I'm late." Sedrick stood, dropping enough cash for both meals plus a tip. "But if you tell anybody I'm getting soft, them baby pictures are going up. I'll write the captions."

I stuffed the extra back in his pocket. "I got the tip. And don't threaten me."

"Ask about me, baby bro."

After he left, I pulled up the Coalition website. The Circuit2Soul Gala was even bigger than he'd let on. Every major Atlanta tech company was sponsoring. Decision makers, potential clients, people who could help me build something real, all in one room in their formal finest.

Sounded like a perfect night for networking. Definitely no need for a date.

Although...

Opal briefly crossed my mind, but I pushed her back out. The idea of smoothing those sharp edges was tempting —I loved a good challenge. But I had a business to build and no time to waste chasing a woman who did not want to be caught.

The cold hit me when I stepped outside. I tucked the scarf into my coat and shoved my hands deep in my pockets for the short walk home.

On the way, I was already mentally conceding that Sedrick had a point. Putting down roots, making a real home here, at least for now, was not a bad idea.

It felt good to be home.

Chapter Four

O^{pal}

I liked to break up hours of solitude with the energy of other people around me. Coffee Theory's lunchtime crowd offered the perfect mix of noise and activity—office workers hunting caffeine fixes, students sprawled across tables with laptops, tourists consulting their phones about their next destination. I often packed up my work and settled in among them when I wanted controlled chaos instead of silence.

Asia sat across from me, alternating between bites of her colorful salad and sharing her thoughts about wedding venues. I savored my turkey club, letting the combination of crisp bacon and creamy avocado make up for only having coffee that morning.

"And I mean, I love her like my own mom, but I already know Jordan's mom is going to try to run this whole thing,"

Asia said, propping one elbow on the table. "But my mom and I are not having it. They can plan the honeymoon." She paused, reconsidering. "Well... maybe not that either."

"Maybe the reception?"

Asia scowled. "No. That's literally part of the wedding, Opal."

"Well, excuse me. I've literally never planned a wedding." I bit off more of my sandwich and scowled back.

Asia leaned forward, a conspiratorial gleam in her eye. "You know something about dinner at Marcel, don't you?"

"What do you mean?" I stole a cherry tomato from her salad and popped it into my mouth, aiming for casual. I'd already promised Jordan I would be there to witness the proposal, but keeping his secrets from Asia was becoming harder by the day.

Asia's manicured nails tapped an excited rhythm on the tabletop. "Never mind, I want to be surprised. I just don't want any empty spots at that table."

"You're already annoying and you're not even engaged yet." I took a long sip of iced tea, stalling before the inevitable interrogation.

"No luck finding a date for dinner? Or the gala?"

I met her pointed stare head-on. "I'm not bringing a date to the gala. I'll be working. And I'm definitely not dragging some random person to your potential engagement dinner on Valentine's Day. I want to celebrate with you. Don't make it weird."

Asia's full lips formed a playful pout. "It doesn't have to be a date-date. What about that cute guy from Soul Cycle?"

"The gay one who's practically engaged to the instructor?" I giggled. "He would at least be comic relief."

"There has to be someone. Nobody at work?"

"Please change the subject."

"What about your neighbor? The one with... what is that dog? A Maltese?"

"Sixty years old, Asia."

"Really?" The 'v' between her arched brows deepened. "Black really don't crack, does it?" She threw up her hands. "You're not making this easy. I just want everything to be perfect."

"I know you do, friend." I reached across the table to squeeze her hand. "I want you focused on having an amazing time, not worrying about who I'm sitting next to. I'm truly happy for you and Jordan. I don't need a date to make the night special."

Asia's shoulders dropped. "I want you to be happy too. You deserve someone amazing."

Her heart was in the right place, even if her methods were misguided and relentless. "I appreciate you thinking of me, but I have my own plan for my life. I am happy. I have a career, great friends, healthy family, my independence. I don't need a man to complete me."

"Nobody said anything about completing you." Asia speared a cucumber with her fork. "You're a strong, independent woman who don't need no man. But your back needs to be blown out every so often. A guy that likes you a lot and will take you to the movies with some poundtown action afterward wouldn't suck."

"You talk like a fifteen-year-old on an Omegle chat, Asia."

"I think I'm just hungry."

"Eat your damn salad."

The café door swung open and Sterling walked in looking like he'd stepped straight off a GQ cover, the business-casual edition in slacks and a short sleeved polo that showed off well-formed biceps. His gut-level laughter carried across the space as he joked with Joya.

"Earth to Opal." Asia's voice snapped me back. Her eyes were wide, eyebrows reaching for her hairline. "You good over there?"

"What? Nothing." I focused intently on rescuing a slice of avocado that was escaping my sandwich.

"Who is that fine piece of man you're pretending not to notice? You're practically drooling."

I'd never been more grateful for my dark skin as a column of heat blazed up one side of my neck. "He's a tenant in the building. I've seen him around sometimes."

"That's all?" Asia's voice dripped skepticism. "Your eyes are about to pop out of your head. There's definitely a story there."

"We've talked a couple of times. He seems nice. I barely know him."

"Whatever. You're blushing like a teenager with her first crush."

"I do not blush." But my cheeks were definitely heated. I risked another glance at Sterling. As if he'd been waiting for me to notice him, he raised a hand in a wave. My stomach did a little flip as I nodded back before quickly looking away.

"Opal. Did you hear anything I just said?"

"Sorry, what?"

"Never mind. You're gone."

"I'm right here."

"So is he." Asia nodded toward Sterling. "And that's exactly the problem."

"Asia, I barely know him."

"Your face says parts of you would like to know him

better. Don't even try to deny it. I haven't seen you this interested in anyone since—"

"We don't need to talk about him."

My last serious relationship had imploded two years ago. Since then, I'd focused on my career, on building a life where my worth wasn't tied to becoming someone's wife. Sterling's ability to wreck my nerves with just his presence was making that goal significantly harder.

Asia looked pained. "Sorry. I forgot."

"It's fine." I waved her off with a forced smile. "Ancient history. I just don't give him any of my energy anymore."

"You know you don't have to be a strong Black woman all the time. You're allowed to have a soft life."

"Yes, honey. I know. Can we focus on your dinner?"

"Maybe I'm having too much fun watching you look at this man like he's Aaron Pierre in that JHud video."

"He's just a tenant who works a few floors above me. We ran into each other yesterday when the café was closed and he bought me lunch because we both missed the lunch cutoff. That's all."

One eyebrow rose higher. "That man is fine as wine. He's been watching you this whole time, and now he's headed this way."

"What do you—" The words died in my throat as Sterling appeared at our table. Asia's whole face lit up like Times Square.

"Ladies," he rumbled, his voice oozing over us like honey. "I apologize for interrupting. I saw Opal and wanted to say hello."

"We don't mind at all," Asia chirped before I could speak. "I'm Asia, Opal's best friend. And you are...?"

"Sterling Carter." He offered his hand. "It's a pleasure to meet you."

Asia's grin widened as they shook hands. "Sterling. I love that name. It's so... Black classic. Like Harlem Renaissance. Do you have siblings with similar names?"

Sterling laughed. "My brother's name is Sedrick. He's still mad I got the better name."

"So... are you new to the building? I'm here pretty often and I'd remember seeing you around."

"I am. Yesterday was my first day in the building." His eyes flicked to mine briefly. "I just relocated from New York."

I found myself holding my breath, hyper-aware of his presence. The energy in the room shifted whenever he was near. His cologne—subtle, woodsy, masculine—made me want to lean closer just to breathe him in.

Asia, ever the opportunist, pounced. "Well, welcome to Atlanta! How is your wife adjusting to life in the South?"

Sterling chuckled, his knowing look suggesting he saw right through her. "It's just me, and I was actually born and raised here. I'm settling back in just fine."

I watched the exchange, torn between mortification and fascination. Part of me wanted to melt into the floor while another part hung on his every word. I felt Asia's excitement building as she processed the fact that he was single.

Too late, I realized where she was going.

"You know, my man and I are hosting dinner at Marcel this Friday evening. Opal doesn't have a date and she won't let me fix her up with anyone. You should come—our treat, of course."

My eyes went wide with panic. Before I could jump in, Sterling spoke. "Wow, Marcel. That's very kind of you to offer—"

"Sterling!" Joya's voice cut through the café. "Proper iced Ethiopian for Sterling!"

He glanced over his shoulder. "I'm sorry, I need to run. It was lovely meeting you, Asia. Opal, always a pleasure." With a smile and a wave, he retrieved his coffee and headed out.

"Asia."

"Hmmm?" She answered, stabbing at her now wilted salad.

I glared at her, even more irritated. "Did you suddenly develop a debilitating fever that made you invite him to accompany me to my best friend's potential engagement dinner?"

"Of course I invited him." She waved off my protest. "He's handsome, friendly, available, and he obviously likes you. He came all the way over here—"

"Twenty whole steps."

"—just to say hi. He's so... *chalant*. You know what I mean? Like, not leaving things up to chance?"

I buried my face in my hands with a groan. "I don't think that's a word, but what does that have to do with you asking him out for me? This is your worst idea ever. And I'm including the time we crashed your ex's wedding."

"That was epic." Asia paused, considering. "Okay, maybe objecting to the marriage because he broke up with me over email was immature. But it was fun and they didn't even kick us out."

I let my silence speak for itself.

"Sterling seems different from your usual type."

"You've known him two minutes," I pointed out, though she wasn't wrong.

"Men aren't that complicated," Asia countered. "I have a good picker. There's something there, if you'd let yourself see it."

I pushed my empty plate away with a sigh. "Even if

there was... something... which I'm not admitting to, I'm not ready for it. I don't have time for whatever it is."

Asia's face took on a serious expression as she leaned in, beaming her big greenish-brown eyes into mine. "It's been two years, Opal. I'll stand by you as long as I need to but how much longer are you going to let a bad breakup hold you back? Kellan has moved on, dated other people, gotten married, and you're—"

"Doing just fine. The mark of a good life isn't laying up under some selfish oaf who steals my ideas and makes hella money off of them. I don't give a fuck how great Kellan is doing."

A familiar ache spread through my chest at the mention of my ex. I'd thought he was the one, right up until I discovered he'd violated my trust and taken all my notes and ideas to his company. A year later, his app was taking off and he was reaping the benefits of my hard work. The betrayal still stung.

"Okay, okay." She threw her hands up in surrender. "I'm dropping it. I'm sorry. I... just... don't miss out on something potentially amazing because Kellan was a dick and a thief."

The tension in her face eased into a smile, then widened to a grin. "Besides, I know you. I know what you like, and I know you've been thinking about letting that man drip sweat all over you."

I couldn't help my laughter. "You're awful and annoying. Don't you have work to do?"

Asia gathered her barely touched salad and grabbed her bag, then paused. "You know... if I was really awful, I'd tell you that if you don't invite Sterling to dinner, I'll have to ask Elliott to join us. I'm sure he'd be thrilled to bore you all evening."

"You are the devil incarnate."

"You'll thank me later." Asia scrunched up her nose and gave an innocent shrug, then pressed a quick kiss to my cheek and breezed out of the café with her phone already at her ear.

The thought of spending an entire evening next to Jordan's frat brother, listening to them bark and throw up hand signs and reminisce about college made my skin crawl.

"Empty threats," I muttered. "I hope."

* * *

My mouth dropped open in a long, drawn-out yawn as I stepped inside the elevator. It was just after eight o'clock but I'd made so much progress on clearing tickets on the platform that I could model the demo at the status meeting in the morning. I was exhausted but extremely proud.

"I heard that," said a familiar voice in a conciliatory tone.

I jumped, screaming, "Shit!" so loud I scared myself. In the corner of the elevator, just out of my peripheral vision, was Sterling. He wore a long wool coat and had a dark, cozy scarf tucked into it.

The elevator door slid closed, leaving Sterling and me in a bubble of charged silence.

"Sorry," he said. "I keep doing that to you. I guess I'm quiet."

"Yeah, well. If you apologize with lunch again, I won't complain. That chicken Philly was delicious."

"It was. I enjoyed it so much, they might see me again."

My fingers fidgeted with the strap of my leather messenger bag, my eyes fixed on the illuminated floor numbers as we descended. As usual, I felt the change in energy when he was in a room and his presence made me hyperaware of the square footage of the confined space.

Sterling cleared his throat. "Long day?"

I nodded, glancing at him briefly. "Twelve-hour days are standard at this point in my project. Lots of deadlines and meetings. Not enough hours."

"Mmmm," Sterling hummed, his smile sympathetic. "What exactly are you working on? Must be something significant to demand those kinds of hours."

"I'm lead developer on a Diversity, Equity, and Inclusion platform. We're building a tool that goes beyond basic reporting. I want to create systemic change from jump for employers. And employees."

His eyebrows rose, genuine interest replacing his casual curiosity. "Important work, especially now."

"Agreed," I said. "Especially in this climate where it needs to be done, but nobody wants to do it. I guess I'm one of the few that feel lucky that this is what I feel led to do."

"One of the things I was happy to leave behind when I left the corporate world," Sterling said. "More to be done and no one else to do it."

"So you're not a corporate drone like me?"

"Yes, but of my own doing and not an overlord in the corner office. I work in public relations. I thought it was time to spread my wings and offer my talents to the general public. I like the flexibility of having several clients and signing my own paycheck."

I sighed. "That does sound nice."

As the elevator reached the parking garage level, Sterling stepped forward, holding the door open with one hand. "After you," he said, gesturing for me to exit first.

"Thank you," I murmured, stepping out into the dimly lit underground space. I dug my key fob out of my bag and had taken only a few steps when Sterling's voice stopped me.

"Opal. About earlier..." he began, his tone hesitant. Then he noticed something and paused. "You're not wearing a coat. It's thirty-seven degrees out here."

Before I could respond, Sterling unwrapped his scarf and looped it around my neck. "I want that back. It was a gift from my mother."

"Thank you," I said, surprised by the unexpected gesture. "And... I apologize about earlier. I was not expecting Asia to ambush you with an invite. She means well, but subtlety isn't her strong suit."

"Seems an accurate description," Sterling said. "I sensed you were uncomfortable with her inviting me to dinner, so I thought it best to wait and let you extend the invitation yourself. If you wanted to."

"Oh..." I didn't know what to do with this man who had forethought and consideration for the feelings of others. It was a turn-on, that was for sure. "I appreciate that. It's complicated. Asia's convinced her boyfriend is going to propose at this dinner and she's determined to have a full table of couples to witness the blessed event."

Sterling nodded, almost smiling. "And... you're not sure if you want to bring someone along for the pressure of that kind of intimate gathering?"

"Exactly," I agreed, relieved that he understood. "I'm sure I would enjoy your company. It's just—"

"Marcel is a lot for a first date." Sterling finished for me, his eyes twinkling with amusement. "Not sure I can go up from there."

I laughed, feeling some of the tension dissipate. "You feel me."

Sterling took a step closer, the playful glint in his eyes

softening. His shoulders squared slightly, and the hint of a smile pulled at the corner of his mouth. "For the record, I have no plans. I would be honored to accompany you and give you someone to laugh with when the couples make their syrupy toasts to each other. It's completely up to you, but consider me an option if you're comfortable with the idea. No pressure, I promise."

I hated to admit it, but I was a goner. The sincerity in his dark brown eyes and the gentility of his tone... and the softness of his scarf did me in.

What is this, cashmere?

"It's freezing out here and you don't have a coat on. How about you take tonight to think about it and we can talk about it in the morning at the cafe?"

I smiled, feeling a weight lift from my shoulders. "That sounds perfect, actually. Thank you. For the scarf and for understanding."

Sterling glanced around the garage, checking from one end to the other. "Would you like me to walk you to your car?"

For a moment, I was tempted to accept, just to prolong our conversation. But I shook my head, gesturing towards my Audi Q5 just steps away from the elevator. "I'm parked right over there. One of the perks of being an early bird."

Sterling's brows rose in appreciation. "Nice ride." He pointed to a Range Rover a few spots down from me. "That's me."

"Like minds," we said in unison, then burst into laughter at the coincidence.

As our laughter faded, I found myself reluctant to end the moment. Before I could make it weird, I said, "Well. I should get going. Thanks again."

Sterling nodded. "Of course. I'll see you in the morning?"

We parted ways, each heading to our respective vehicles. I chanced a glance back over my shoulder. Sterling was doing the same, and our eyes met. We shared a final wave before getting into our cars.

My analytical mind was already working overtime, running the pros and cons.

On one hand, navigating a Valentine's Day dinner with someone I barely knew sounded like the stuff of nightmares. What if it was awkward?

On the other hand... Asia was right. I'd had plenty of daydreams about that man in particular dripping sweat all over me.

Chapter Five

S terling

The usual crowd hadn't yet hit the coffee shop when I arrived. The strum of an acoustic guitar played through the speakers over the empty café while early morning light filtered through the foggy windows.

Joya was behind the counter as usual, half-turned toward me while moving through her opening routine.

"Proper ethiopian, right?" she asked, already reaching for the jar of coarse-ground beans.

"Exactly," I said, pulling my phone from the pocket of my overcoat. "And add one more... uhhh..." I rolled my eyes up, trying to remember Opal's exact order. "Precise americano... what else did she say..."

"Extra hot, half pump hazelnut, splash of half-and-half?" Joya grinned. "Must be trying to get on Opal's good side."

"Something like that. We're actually meeting to discuss something. I thought I'd go ahead and grab our orders before the line gets long."

"That's thoughtful of you," Joya said, her fingers flying over the iPad. "How are you adjusting to The Avian?"

"It's only been a few days, but I guess I'm falling into a nice rhythm. I've worked in my share of high-rises. It's understood that the, uh... tenants make the experience."

"Don't I know it." Joya moved with fluid precision at the espresso machine, barely glancing at what her hands were doing. "Speaking of tenants," she said, dropping her voice and nodding toward the door.

Opal had just entered in tailored steel-grey slacks, a black button-up blouse, a cropped leather jacket and my cashmere scarf. I caught myself thinking it suited her better than it had ever suited me.

"Morning, Opal. Sterling has your order all taken care of. I'll have your coffees ready in just a few minutes. You get your choice of tables since you're so early."

Opal smiled, slowly unwrapping the scarf from around her neck and folding it. "I'd better give this back before I get used to it. Though, I'd love to know where you got it."

"Keep it for now," I told her, pushing it back toward her. "My mother made it."

"Your mother knit this? Wow, she's talented."

I smiled, watching Opal's fingers trace the patterns in the wool. "Yeah, she's always been crafty and she's really gotten into fiber arts since she semi-retired. Something to do in between curating exhibits for the gallery she works with. I think Dad's just happy she's not redecorating the house anymore."

"It is a cheaper hobby. My mother tries to change the

paint color in the den every spring. Dad pretends not to hear her."

I gestured to a pair of chairs by the window. "Joya should have our coffee in a minute. Let's have a seat—unless you need to rush upstairs?"

Opal settled into one of the chairs. "I can spare a few minutes. How's the renovation of your office space coming along?"

"It's taking longer than we thought it would. It was supposed to be complete before I even arrived in Atlanta. I wasn't trying to leave New York until I had a place to work. It'll be another three weeks, at least. The temporary space works fine, I guess. I'm just ready to work in an office that's mine. Arrange my art. Use my own furniture."

"At least the views are decent." Opal smirked.

"More than decent," I agreed.

"Um... okay, so about Friday—"

"Here you go," Joya interrupted, dropping two lidded cups and a container on the table between us. "And just because I know Opal likes my croissants, these are on the house. Enjoy." She stepped away before either of us could protest.

I opened the box, angling it toward Opal. She took a croissant, her fingers breaking apart the flaky layers and popping a bite into her mouth. The small sound of pleasure she made sent heat straight through me, more than I needed before eight AM.

"You were saying something about Friday?" I asked, trying to focus on the conversation and not the way her lips curved around the pastry.

She brushed her hands together, shaking the flakes from her fingers. "I just want to be crystal clear. Asia is my very best friend, and this dinner is really important. Jordan thinks she has no idea he's proposing to her. I wouldn't miss this dinner for the world. I need to be there for her big moment."

"I hear a big ol' but coming."

Opal sighed, rolling her eyes. "She's inviting all these couples. And... me. The pressure is on to find someone to go with so I don't have to sit in the middle of a nightmare with some guy she picks out for me. They'll all be swooning and making eyes at each other. I'm not even joking. And it's not that I'll be lonely or anything, just painfully uncom-fortable."

"Understood. No one should have to endure lovey-dovey eyes and cutesy names alone. But it's not like you need a date to have a good time."

"True. It's just... I don't want to feel like the odd man out. And honestly, I don't think Asia wants that for me either, as misguided as her attempt to find me a date might be. I don't want you to feel obligated to come to dinner because Asia ambushed you. There are so many things you could be doing instead."

"There's also nothing wrong with two single people providing emotional backup while surrounded by couples overdosing on romance."

She studied me over her coffee cup. "So... you'd really be okay with that? Being backup?"

I chuckled. "I was solo dolo when Sedrick proposed to my sister-in-law, Blair, so I know what it's like to be in the middle of a crowd doing one thing and I'm out here doing a whole different thing. Besides," I added, "then we both avoid the pressure of finding a date for the night and we get a great steak dinner out of it. I haven't been to Marcel in over a decade."

Opal paused like she had something to say, but unlike

the other day, she hesitated. I gestured with a hand that she should let it out.

"So... forgive me for however this comes off. You... I mean... you're a *nice* looking man. And I mean this in the most not-flirting-at-all way possible—how do you not have plans? It's Valentine's Day."

I couldn't help but laugh. It wasn't the first time someone had asked me how I was single, and I doubted it would be the last.

"Well. Thank you, I think, for the compliment, first of all. I feel like I've worked hard for that. Second, I guess you could say my love life is also under construction. Seriously, you'd only be keeping me from a Slim & Husky's pizza and catching up on my Netflix queue."

I was momentarily caught by the rich brown of her eyes. "I'm wide open, but if you'd rather keep things simple, I completely understand."

She finished the last bite of her croissant and pulled a ringing phone from her bag. "No, I'm definitely taking you up on your offer," she said, pressing a button to silence the device. She picked up her coffee, the scarf, and her bag. "I think I'm getting pulled into a meeting, so I'm going to head to my office, but we should go over details."

I pulled a cardholder from my breast pocket, slipped a business card out, and handed it to her. "Shoot me a text or an email. We should have each other's contact information anyway."

"Sounds good. Thank you, Sterling. You're helping more than you know."

I watched her leave the shop, then wait for the elevator and step inside. I'd been staring longer than I meant to when Joya appeared with a white cloth to wipe down the table.

"Not for nothing, but you two look good together."

I raised an eyebrow, aiming for casual. "I don't think that's on Opal's agenda. Though I wouldn't mind exploring it."

Joya's smile lingered as she moved to another table. I drained my coffee cup and pulled out my phone. Opal had only been gone a few minutes—not enough time to text or email me.

I grabbed a refill of coffee and took the elevator up to my office. Across the courtyard, Opal sat at her desk in a leather executive chair. She glanced up as if sensing I was watching. I lifted my coffee in greeting. She waved back.

The phone vibrated in my pocket. I pulled it out and swiped Sedrick's smug face away. "Whatcha got? Condo or house this time?"

"Neither, man. Your list is so specific, it's taking some time to narrow down options I know you'll look at. I got it coming, but Blair and I were talking about tomorrow night. Why don't you come by and hang with Shaw?"

"Hang with Shaw?" I repeated, confused. "Shaw doesn't need a sitter. He should be hanging out somewhere being awkward and smiling in somebody's face like his corny ass daddy. Where are you and Blair going?"

"Some spot called The Garden Room that Blair wants to try out. All I know is if I see one of them grass Instagram walls, I'm out. I ain't trying that hard."

"Liar," I argued, laughing. "You talk tough, but you will pose in front of a grass wall and you will like it."

"You don't know me, man. So I'm supposed to tell your nephew that Uncle Sterling ain't coming to buy him a pizza and hang with him? He said y'all could play some game he's into. I told him you're probably too old to know which buttons to push."

"He's talking about NBA2K. I crushed him the last time we played. And as much as I love showing my nephew up, I'm working on a little something."

"Working on what? With who?"

"I ain't telling you shit."

"Wait—hold up. You met somebody? Already?" The excitement pitched his voice higher, making me chuckle. "Come on, tell big bro. Who is she? What's her name? What does she do?"

"I ain't got to tell you shit. Next thing I know, I'll be getting a call from Ma. Already risking it by telling you I have plans. Matter of fact—bye, Sedrick."

"Sterling Everett Carter, do not hang up—Blair! Sterling talmbout he got a date tomorrow. Yeah, already!"

"Have a good time tomorrow," I said, then added, "Tag me in the pics you swear you're not taking."

"He won't tell me who," I heard Sedrick telling Blair in the background. "Baby, talk to him! See if you can get—"

I ended the call, grinning. My phone immediately vibrated with a text:

> This ain't over, punk.

Chapter Six

O^{pal}

I arrived at Marcel thirty minutes early, my hand pressed against my stomach where nerves danced a frantic rhythm. My anxiety hummed at a pitch that could shatter glass. The romantic mood inside the restaurant, all wood and copper and a wall of expensive wines, wasn't helping.

I was more of a lounge girl. Give me comfortable couches, small plates, hits from the 80s and 90s playing from speakers overhead at reasonable decibels. The kind of place where a random song would trigger muscle memory, and suddenly everyone would magically remember dance moves from years ago, even if they couldn't remember where they'd parked their car earlier.

I pushed out a shaky breath as I looked around for Sterling. I was silently cursing Jordan for setting up Asia's engagement this way. I wanted to see my best friend get engaged. I did not want to be sat in the middle of coupled-up bliss. At least I had a partner in crime.

Over email the previous day, Sterling and I had formed a game plan. We would arrive early, sit at the bar for a few minutes and enjoy a drink—or two—let the atmosphere breathe, get used to each other's company outside the office. I couldn't believe he'd agreed to accompany a complete stranger to dinner to save her from being set up with the world's most boring man's boring frat brother.

Don't get me wrong...I loved Jordan like I loved my third cousin twice removed. He was Asia's dream come true, and she was so ready to be Mrs. Jordan Hale, so if this is what she wanted, I was happy to be there for her.

I found him nestled in a cozy corner of the bar, looking like he'd been poured into a black suit designed by someone who truly understood male anatomy.

"I appreciate you meeting me early," I said, sliding into the booth, my shoulders already dropping. "Consider this an anxiety-management session."

"Glad to be of service," he said, with a resolute nod that managed to be both reassuring and slightly amusing. "I don't live far and I got here faster than I thought I would. What are you having?"

"Manhattan. Extra dry." The words came out more like a command than a request.

Sterling raised a hand to signal the waitstaff. His sleeve pulled back, revealing the glint of an expensive watch. A young man in a burgundy vest appeared as if conjured by magic, crisp white shirt pristine against the dim overhead lighting.

"Two Manhattans," Sterling ordered. "Extra dry, and keep them coming."

I raised an eyebrow, my nervous energy finding an outlet in sass. "Planning on getting me drunk?"

"We both need to be adequately loose for the evening ahead."

The drinks arrived, the amber liquid catching the low bar lights. I took a generous sip, feeling whiskey burn a path down my throat and into the pit of my belly. Bitters and vermouth joined to create a welcome distraction from this entire evening.

"So." Sterling leaned in, his dark eyes sparkling. "What's our game plan for surviving this gauntlet of sweet nothings and romantic activity?"

I swirled the Manhattan, watching the liquid create a tiny whirlpool. "Maybe...we make a game out of how many times we hear certain terms of endearment."

"I like it," he replied, after a sardonic chuckle. "A point each? Anything that's not a proper name goes—love, honey, babe... bae. You take the ladies, I'll take the guys. The person with the highest tally at the end of the night buys the other lunch next week."

I smiled, taking another swig of my cocktail. The alcohol hummed through my veins while Sterling's charm dulled the sharp edges of my anxiety.

This might actually be fun.

Asia arrived like a supernova, radiant in a crimson satin gown that clung to her hips. Platinum and diamond jewelry winked in the light of the chandelier. Jordan trailed her, looking dapper in a dark suit and a fierce lineup, his hand resting on the small of her back.

"There's the happy couple."

Sterling followed my gaze, his eyes widening slightly. "Wow. They know how to make an entrance."

"That's Asia for you. She's never done anything halfway."

I slid out of the booth and stood, wrapping Asia in a long, tight hug. I felt her nerves vibrating through the thin dress, the tension humming just beneath the surface. I pulled back, pressed my forehead to hers, and held her hands. "Tonight will be amazing. You look absolutely stunning, Jordan is handsome AF, and this meal is about to be off every available chain. You got this."

"As expensive as this is going to be, I had better be getting engaged tonight. Know what I'm saying? And...oh —" She stole a glance at Sterling before tucking me in close. "Would it be inappropriate of me to point out that Sterling is wearing. that. suit?"

"I don't think so," I replied with a grin. "I don't think so at all."

"If this turns into something, I'm totally taking credit," she said, leaning in to whisper. "Best. Matchmaker. Ever."

"Yeah, but nothing's gonna—"

"Hey, Keith! Tanya!" Asia waved as a couple approached. "I'm so glad you made it!"

As the group settled at the table, I leaned in to whisper to Sterling. "Some intel—Keith was in Jordan's study cohort in med school. He brought Jordan into the clinic where they all work now. Tara is a pediatric nurse. They've been together since undergrad."

The next couple arrived, and I repeated the pattern. "Matthew is Jordan's line brother. They're Kappas. He's actually going to be one of the groomsmen. Jasmine works in marketing—she and Asia bonded over their love of vintage Black fashion."

Sterling hummed, nodding. "I could have guessed she was into fashion."

"Asia works in communications and freelances as a stylist. It's how she and Jordan met, actually. She was hired to style him for a photo shoot when he joined the clinic."

"Love at first sight, and every sight thereafter," said Jordan, dropping a kiss on Asia's nose. "Love you, babe."

She beamed, melting into him. "Thanks, boo. Love you back."

Ugh. A tie.

Dinner unfolded amid a slightly awkward but bearable rhythm of conversation. We had been arranged strategically with couples nestled together and Sterling and I occupying the middle ground. While topics ranged from date night locales and daycare options, Sterling and I discussed the wine list and amenities at The Avian.

"So, Sterling," Jordan began, cutting through his iceberg wedge salad, "You're new to the group. Tell us what keeps you busy. You know, the usual interrogation."

"Babe, I told you—he just relocated to Atlanta. He has an office in Opal's building."

"I remember, honey. I wanted to let the man tell his own story."

"Well..." Sterling began, "I have indeed just relocated to Atlanta, as Asia mentioned. I've been in New York since I got out of grad school—"

"Where you went for..." Matthew asked, scraping his bowl of lobster bisque like he was trying to get every bite.

"Public Relations. I've been working my way up the chain ever since. I was recently in strategy until my firm did some strategizing of their own and eliminated my role. My folks are getting up there in age and I have some family here, so I made the move. I decided to set something up for myself."

Sterling shrugged, sipping the last of his water. A waiter appeared immediately to refill it.

"So you're starting your own PR firm?" Jordan asked. "Gotta be nerve-wracking to be leaving the corporate world right now."

Sterling's smile was equal parts charming and self-deprecating. "That's one way to put it. I'd say terrifying. Really gets the blood pumping in a way that work in the corporate world never did for me."

The table laughed. I watched, fascinated by how easily he navigated the social terrain. Most men would have either boasted or deflected. Sterling found the perfect middle ground.

I leaned in, whispering, "You're doing so good! You're like...a social ninja."

Sterling raised an eyebrow. "This is what I do, you know. Create in-roads, relate to people."

"I know. It's just...most men would have drowned in awkward, unfunny jokes by now."

"See, I tried that the other day and I got the Opal Richardson stare. I don't dare try that again."

Filets, green beans, smashed potatoes and candied carrots served with a robust cabernet were the main course. I noticed the other couples sharing bites off each other's plates and exchanging looks of affection that made my stomach churn. Whether it was from envy or nausea remained to be seen.

Sterling, to his credit, kept up the charade beautifully, his hand resting casually on the back of my chair. "Need me to create a diversion with the bread basket?" he murmured. "You're very quiet."

I giggled. "I'm fine. I'm just...I can't help analyzing the

table. Valentine's Day is fascinating. So much performative romance."

His laugh was low, just for me. "Performative? Say more."

"I just notice things," I whispered. "They seem like they're all in a contest to out-romance each other. The pressure to appear madly in love, to show it in grand gestures not only for your partner, but for the public."

"You're not into Valentine's Day, then?"

"It's fine as a holiday." I picked up my wine glass, then thought better of it and switched it for water. "The expected charades, the public display of affection seems exhausting. I'd much rather be myself. Show affection and care for my person all year-round. Don't just save it up for this one day so we can prove to people we're in love."

"Mmm," Sterling hummed. "That's deep. I think I'd rather have that, too. But...sometimes folks really are that in love and it's not a charade. Sometimes it's a proud display of a good, strong bond."

"Maybe so," I said, noting I sounded like a Scrooge. It wasn't Sterling's fault that the last man I'd dated seriously, cohabitated with, was practically engaged to, chose Valentine's Day to drop the news that he'd taken my idea for an app and developed it behind my back. He'd claimed it was planned as a surprise to me, but my name was nowhere to be found on the paperwork. It certainly wasn't on the check.

I scooted away the memory of a teary, upsetting dinner to realize Jordan was regaling the table with the story about how he and Asia met. All but Sterling had heard it a hundred times. Asia listened as if hearing it for the first time, her hand resting on his arm.

"You're rolling your eyes," Sterling observed quietly.

"You're really not a fan of love? Or are you just annoyed at this situation?"

"I am a fan of love, actually," I admitted. "I think love is great. When it's genuine. Not superficial and not a show. I don't have time or patience for something that isn't real and I don't think I can risk..."

My voice trailed off. I caught myself before I said too much. Sterling didn't insist that I continue.

Definitely switching to water.

When the dessert course arrived, a decadent four-layer chocolate creation, the romantic overtures reached a crescendo. Couples shared bites, fingers intertwined, whispered conversations punctuated by laughter.

Jordan ordered champagne for the table. When the glasses arrived, he lifted his in a toast. "To good friends and great company. I'm so touched you're all here for the most important night of our lives."

Something in his voice made Asia's eyes widen. She glanced around the table, then back at him. "Babe..."

Jordan set down his glass and reached for her hand. The entire table went still. Even the usual dining room chatter seemed to fade away.

"Asia Montgomery." Jordan's voice carried just enough to draw attention from nearby tables. "You are the most amazing woman I've ever known. You make every day brighter just by being in it."

"Oh my God." Asia's free hand flew to her mouth. "It's happening!"

Jordan slid from his chair to one knee while he pulled a small velvet box from a jacket pocket. "I couldn't imagine my life without you in it. And I don't want to. I need you, I love you, I desperately want you to say you'll marry me."

A stunning oval diamond in a vintage-inspired setting

caught the light. Asia's eyes filled with tears as Jordan slipped it onto her finger.

"Yes," she managed to squeak out. "Of course, yes!"

The dining room erupted in applause. Asia threw her arms around Jordan's neck, nearly knocking them both over. Glasses clinked. Someone ordered more champagne.

I felt Sterling's hand tap my knee under the table. His eyes met mine with gentle concern.. Understanding.

"To the happy couple," he said, raising his glass.

As the excitement settled, conversations resumed. Asia kept glancing at her hand, catching new angles of sparkle. Jordan couldn't stop grinning.

A deafening clap of thunder echoed through the restaurant. En masse, we all looked toward the windows to see a blinding flash of lightning split the night sky, followed by a deluge of rain so hard it sounded like pellets against the glass.

"Is it just me," I said to Sterling, "or is it getting wild out there?"

"Looks like Mother Nature might be trying to compete with Jordan's proposal."

"It's bad," Jordan muttered, checking his phone. "There's a huge system moving through Atlanta right now. The Weather service declared a severe storm warning."

"Well...should we go?" Asia asked.

"I'm not looking forward to driving home in that," said Jordan, still staring at his phone. "But...waiting it out is just as bad. The model is calling for heavy rain until almost midnight."

Two of the couples decided to chance it and stood, pushing their chairs back. "We want to try to get home before it gets too out of hand. Thank you so much for inviting us."

"Congrats! Let's get together next week—it's never too soon to start your wedding plans!"

Sterling glanced at me, noting the worry that was surely evident on my face. "I should probably get going, too," I said. "I have a ways to go and I can't get stuck downtown."

"I think I'm going to grab us a room close by," said Jordan, tapping through screens. "We're even further out than you, Opal. You're welcome to bunk in."

I peered out the window. The interstate would be a nightmare in this weather, but the idea of sharing a room with a newly engaged couple would also be a nightmare. "Oh... no. I'm definitely not staying downtown. I am going to go before it gets worse."

"I'll walk you to your car," said Sterling, already standing.

As we made our way to the coat check, another crash of thunder shook the building. "Shit!" I jumped, instinctively grabbing Sterling's arm. "Sorry," I muttered, releasing him quickly. "I'm not great with storms."

"No problem. Let's get going."

We collected our coats and stepped out into the sheltered valet area. The rain was coming down in sheets, the wind driving it sideways. Even under the awning, we were getting wet.

"This is unbelievable," I said, pulling my coat tighter around me. "I can barely see across the street."

Sterling frowned. "Look...can I propose a Plan B to driving around in this? You can absolutely say no, but I'd like to at least present an option that isn't sharing a room with two people who are probably ready to get it on."

"I can't believe Jordan even suggested that. What's your plan?"

"I live just a few miles from here. Literally ten minutes,

maybe a bit longer in traffic. Would you like to wait out the storm at my place? We'll watch the weather channel, eat up all my snacks."

Sterling raised his hands in an innocent gesture. "I promise to be very boring and respectful."

I should have politely declined and got a room alone.

Or braved the storm—it was just rain.

Or sat in my car playing Solitaire and listening to Sirius XM while the worst of it blew over.

The rain hammered against the valet awning, punctuated by another clap of thunder as both of our cars arrived. "I'd like that," I heard myself saying instead. "That sounds much better than potentially hydroplaning."

"Agreed. So...follow me? I'll text you my address in case you lose me in traffic."

I followed Sterling's tail lights like a lifeline while the rain pelted my windshield so hard I could barely see, even with the wipers on full speed. I gripped the steering wheel tightly as every few seconds, a flash of lightning lit up the sky, followed by a rumble of thunder.

When we finally pulled into a parking garage under a towering building, I let out a long breath I'd been holding the entire time.

Sterling was waiting for me by my car door. "Made it," he said with a reassuring smile. "Let's get inside before this storm decides to get any worse."

I got out, grabbed my bag and my phone, then tapped out a quick text to Asia to update her.

> Went to Sterling's place to wait out the storm. I'll send you a ping so you know where I am. You know, in case something happens.

> I knew it! J got us a room at the W.

> Enjoy taking that suit off piece by piece.

> Asia! It's not like that. He's being nice. I'm going to let him be nice.

> Mmmhmm. Keep pretending that man doesn't have a thing for you. He sat through that whole dinner with a smile on his face and an arm across your chair.

> I'm not wrong about this and I want credit. FUCK HIM.

I swiped Asia's text away quickly before Sterling could see it.

I think I was too late. He seemed amused as he offered his arm and led me toward the revolving doors.

* * *

Sterling's apartment was exactly what I expected—sophisticated and masculine, yet comfortable. The interior was decorated in muted tones, with tastefully elegant furniture and fixtures, accented by a smattering of modern art perfect for a mid-city condo. The furniture struck a balance between aesthetic appeal and genuine comfort, as I discovered when Sterling gestured for me to take a seat on one of the plush couches. It almost swallowed me up.

"Thank you for offering your place to wait out the weather," I said, reaching down to unbuckle the straps on my heels. Freeing my feet from their leather constraints brought immediate relief. "I can't remember if we've ever had a storm so bad I couldn't drive home."

"Yeah, no problem at all. Make yourself at home." Sterling shrugged off his suit jacket, draping it over one of the chairs in the six-person dining set. "Can I get you something to drink? Water? Juice? Tea? I'm no Joya, but I could brew up some coffee. Or..."

His voice took on a playful lilt as he rubbed his palms together. "I have a decent bottle of red I could open."

"After that drive, wine sounds perfect," I replied, trying —and failing—not to stare as he removed his cuff links with practiced ease, the silver catching the low light before disappearing into his pocket. A movement so simple wouldn't normally stop me in my tracks, but the hint of wiry muscle up his arm made my mouth go dry.

I wiggled my toes and let them sink into the deep pile carpet, then gravitated toward the window again. The storm showed no signs of relenting; if anything, it seemed to be intensifying. Rain washed against the glass in sheets, creating mesmerizing patterns that distorted the city lights beyond.

"You have an incredible view. You can see the whole city from here."

"It's not bad on a night like tonight," Sterling replied, his words punctuated by the pop of a cork.

When he handed me my glass, his fingers brushed against mine, sending an electric current coursing through my body. I took a slow sip, letting the wine bloom across my tongue and spread through my chest like liquid courage.

"That's why I don't mind that Sedrick—that's my brother—is taking his sweet time finding me a place."

"Oh... this isn't yours?" I asked, viewing the space with renewed interest, trying to imagine it stripped of its current sophistication.

"Nah. Temporary. Everything in here except my clothes

and some dishes is borrowed. For what I'm paying, though, and the cost of something really nice? I may as well stay. I'm not cheap, but the prices they're asking don't seem to match up with what they're giving."

"Mmm," I hummed thoughtfully. "I've heard it's tough out there. That's partly why I'm still out in Gwinnett County."

"Gwinnett? Now that's a commute," Sterling said, his hand ghosting over my elbow as he guided me back to the couch. He settled in beside me, setting his wine glass on the coffee table. "If I can be nosy, how'd you end up out there?"

"It wasn't exactly a choice. The guy I'd been dating—who I was actually supposed to marry—lived out there because his aunt left him the house and he didn't want to move out."

"Okay." He nodded. "I get it."

"When we split, I'd just started a new job and had no time to apartment hunt. Asia knew someone who managed an apartment complex and had a vacancy…"

"Was the breakup a long, drawn-out thing? Did he drop it on you out of the blue? It sounds like it was a surprise."

I spat out a bitter pat of laughter. "Oh, no. You are not going to get me to rant about my ex-fiancé tonight."

"It wasn't a trap. I'm just curious how a man fumbles a woman like you."

Chapter Seven

 O^{pal}

I huffed a laugh and took another swig of wine. It was delicious, and I was thirsty, but I needed to tread lightly; otherwise, I'd rant about Kellen all night.

"You become a selfish thief and steal from a person you claimed to want to build a life with."

"*Daaaaaamn*," Sterling commented, rearing back dramatically. "He fucked up."

"Then you lie about it when you're confronted with the evidence that you went behind that person's back to make money off of their intellectual property. At dinner. On Valentine's Day. That's how you fumble me."

"Oh. Fuck. No wonder..."

"Yeah. Ever since then, Asia has mysteriously made sure I've had a great Valentine's Day. She's really a sweetheart."

"She is." Sterling poured wine into his mouth and swallowed. "So what did he steal?" he asked. "Sounds techie."

"An app idea. One of those apps where you plug in where you are and what you want to do, and it hooks you up with a million different options. It could be super local or super global—like say you're going to London and want some ideas off the beaten path. Stuff like that. Reviews, testimonials—you could even book right on the app."

Sterling's eyes widened. "I can see that taking off. Did you get any legal advice?"

I sighed, the memory still fresh despite the time that had passed. "It was my word against his. He had a head start, and all of my notes and by the time I realized what was happening, he'd already launched it. The app blew up, and I couldn't afford the legal battle. It was a bitter pill to swallow."

Sterling nodded sympathetically, his expression thoughtful. "That's rough. But you're doing well now, right? You've moved on."

I shrugged, trying to keep my tone light despite the heaviness in my chest. "I suppose. Except that I'm still in the temporary apartment I moved into two years ago because I couldn't stand to look at his face, let alone live in his house. Thankfully, my project really took off at work. Finding a place to live just kept falling to the bottom of my to-do list."

"I take it you don't love it out in Gwinnett?"

"Oh, yeah, I love that my upstairs neighbors think 3 AM is the perfect time to rearrange furniture. Or practice their dance routines. Or whatever it is they're doing up there." I rolled my eyes. "And the people next door blast true crime podcasts so loud I can recite them word for word. Then they have raunchy sex in between blistering screaming matches."

"That... sounds miserable. At least you can get some peace and quiet at work."

"Uhm... in theory. In reality, ConnectTech likes to play into the work hard, play hard mentality of Silicon Valley. Lots of meetings around the billiards table and monthly birthday celebrations and every other week is some kind of recognition for something. *Donuts in the break room because we went thirty-one days without anyone getting locked out of the SharePoint site* type shit."

Sterling chuckled, his eyes crinkling at the corners. "Sounds like they're trying to keep everyone's spirits up."

I nodded, offering a wry smile. "Maybe. Or it's a way to keep us all in this endless cycle of meetings and celebrations. It's exhausting, and when I'm on a dev deadline, I can't work like that. I was going to quit, but that would fuck up my boss' life entirely, so the compromise is that they pay for co-working space at The Avian."

"Power move." Sterling raised his glass to toast.

"Indeed," I said, grinning and tapping my glass against his. "It gives me the peace and quiet I need to get the job done."

"You seem to be a person that cherishes solitude. It's just you in the office at The Avian, isn't it?"

"I know how I sound. I am introverted and I am spoiled, but I'm not antisocial. I'm... *particular*. By the way, it's creepy that you watch me from your office."

"I'm definitely not trying to be a creep. And when I move to thirty-two, I won't be able to see you."

"Aw." My lips turned down in a pronounced frown. "Just when I was about to develop an elaborate series of hand signals. I could flash my hands three times and you could bring me a chicken Philly."

"I feel like email would work way better. And there's nothing wrong with protecting your peace. In a world that's always buzzing, it's rare to find someone who understands the power of quiet."

"Sounds like you know some loud people, too?" I slid my glass onto the coffee table and curled up on the couch, getting as comfortable as I could in a damp dress.

"Well, you know... there's a stark difference between an office in Manhattan and an office in Midtown, Atlanta. After a while, the noise starts to feel like a constant hum in the background of my life. I like a place where I can think without interruptions, where the only sounds in the background are... me. Talking to myself."

"It's like you're reading my mind," I said in a near whisper. "So... circling back to my comment yesterday about how it's Valentine's Day and you're with me and..." I waved a hand in the air. "And outside is doing that."

Sterling laughed. Then he got serious and kind of quiet. "I gave up a Friday night of doing nothing and falling asleep watching Netflix to eat a free steak next to an intelligent, fascinating, beautiful woman. I think I won."

The compliment was unexpected. It kicked off a chain reaction that I wasn't ready to deal with, and the wine exacerbated. I quickly looked away in an effort to play it cool, despite the fact that Sterling had set my heart rate to gallop.

"Well... I didn't make out so bad myself."

Time slipped away as we talked, the storm providing a rolling backdrop to our conversation. I was surprised at how at ease I felt in his presence, talking, laughing, sharing wine and stories. When my phone vibrated with a text message, I blinked at the screen and gasped.

"Oh, shit. It's nearly midnight. I can't believe I have you up so late." I pulled up the weather radar, grimacing at the massive band of red and yellow moving across the screen like an angry bruise. "I... okay, we're kind of in a break and then it's going to ramp up again. If I go now, I could—"

"Absolutely not." The lines between his eyes betrayed genuine concern. "The roads will be shitty and packed, then the rain will start up again and you'll be stuck trying to get home. I don't mind you being here. Please don't make me worry about you."

"I could make it, though. It's not that bad—" Even as the words left my mouth, lightning split the sky outside, followed by a loud, forceful thunderclap.

Sterling smirked, arching a brow in amusement. "You were saying?"

"Uhm... I was saying I'm gonna sit my ass right here." I laughed at my own stubbornness. "But you should go to bed. I don't want to impose on your space."

"Impose?" He laughed. "Not even close. I have a guest bedroom, though I should warn you, I'm not exactly moved in here yet. There are still boxes everywhere."

"I don't even need a room. I can just curl up on the couch..."

Sterling interrupted me with a grunt and a wave. "You are going to sleep in a bed. First things first, though." He pushed himself up from the couch. "I need to find you something to chill in. You should get out of that dress before it wrinkles beyond repair. Looks expensive."

I smoothed a hand over the fabric that was bunching up around my hips. "Asia picked this out. She thinks I wear too much black."

"Nah. You looked great." Sterling rolled his shoulders in a stretch that made his shirt pull taut across his chest, the fabric outlining every well-defined muscle. "Let me see what I can find so you can properly relax."

The sound of drawers opening and closing came from down the hallway before Sterling reappeared, holding a pair of grey sweats and what looked like a well-loved t-shirt. "The shirt is from my Morehouse undergrad days. Feel honored—it's a favorite. And I found these sweats still new in the package. My mom's always buying me stuff 'just in case.'"

"Just in case you end up with a surprise overnight guest?" I took the clothes, unable to resist running my fingers over the worn cotton of the t-shirt, imagining years of washes that had rendered it to this perfect state. "Your mom sounds like good people."

"The best. Bathroom's down the hall if you need it. Guest room is to the left."

"Thanks." I stood, gathering the clothes in my arms like precious cargo. "If this is turning into a slumber party, we need snacks."

"Oh, say less. I'll dig up something while you get comfortable."

When I returned, feeling deliciously cozy in his borrowed clothes that smelled faintly of fabric softener and something uniquely Sterling, he'd unveiled an elaborate gift basket wrapped in cellophane and tied with a copper bow.

"Bougie snacks," he announced with a flourish, already starting to unwrap it. "The leasing company left this for me when I moved in. They really went all out."

I curled back into my spot on the couch, pulling my feet under me. "What we got?"

Sterling started pulling items out one by one, each new discovery adding to the impromptu feast. "Let's see... buttery crackers, some kind of artisanal cheese spread, chocolate-covered everything..." He held up a jar that caught the dim light. "Local honey?"

I laughed, accepting the box of crackers he passed over. "These look good."

"Can't go wrong with crackers and cheese or chocolate and sea salt." He settled back into his seat, but closer than before—close enough to feel the heat radiating from his body. "Want to find something to watch while we sample these bougie ass snacks?"

"Please, no true crime. I've been listening to Forensic Files through the walls for two years."

Sterling grabbed the remote, turning the TV on with a press of the finger. "No murder. Got it."

"On the bright side, you should call me if you ever need to get away with murder. I think I've noted every mistake a criminal makes."

"You're frightening, Opal."

We scrolled through Netflix options, debating the merits of various standup comedy specials while making our way through the gift basket contents. The chocolate really was good, especially paired with the wine, the flavors melding together on my tongue in a perfect blend of bitter and sweet.

The storm continued its assault outside, but it felt distant now, like background music to our cozy sanctuary.

"Wait, go back," I said when A Different World flashed by in the Netflix menu. "Have you seen they finally added this?"

"Only been binge-watching it every night. I fall asleep to Ms. Aretha singing the theme song." Sterling's grin was infectious, lighting up his whole face. "Which season you want to jump into?"

"Definitely season four. Peak Whitley and Dwayne energy."

"'Baby, please!'" Sterling cried out in a perfect Dwayne Wayne impression that had me dissolving into laughter. "That scene was all ad-lib."

"I heard that. The way he busts in and breaks through the crowd." I shook my head, remembering the iconic moment. "Whitley really had that man doing the most."

"While also doing the most," Sterling teased, scrolling to the episode. "The way she'd whine 'Dwaaaayne' every time he got on her nerves."

As the episodes played, we kept up a running commentary, quoting favorite lines. The wine and laughter had created a bubble around us, and I found myself relaxing more deeply than I had in months, maybe years.

"You know what this night needs?" Sterling said during a quiet moment. "Please tell me you're a popcorn person."

"Is there any other kind of person to be?"

He disappeared into the kitchen, and I heard the homey sounds of cabinets opening and closing. "Butter, or plain?"

"Is that even a real question? Butter!"

His laugh drifted back to me. "A woman after my own heart."

The microwave hummed to life, and soon the aroma of popcorn filled the apartment, making my mouth water. When Sterling returned with a big bowl, he sat so our bodies were touching, his solid form against my side. I felt the contact from shoulder to knee, and I didn't mind at all. When I shifted to get more comfortable, his hand landed on my knee. Just for a moment to steady himself as he reached for his wine glass, but the brief contact sent sparks racing through me that had nothing to do with the storm or the wine.

"I can't believe you still know all these lines," Sterling said.

"You need to be saying that to yourself." I reached for more popcorn at the same time he did, our fingers brushing in the bowl. Neither of us pulled away immediately, the simple touch becoming far more intimate than it should have been. "You've been slipping up on some of the best parts, though."

"That's because I was distracted." His eyes met mine, and the intensity in them made me swallow hard. "Still am, actually."

The show was forgotten, faded into the background. Dialogue and the canned laugh track became white noise. Sterling's arm ended up resting along the back of the couch behind me, not quite touching but close enough that I could feel its presence like a whisper against my skin. Every small movement brought us a fraction closer together, the air between us growing thick.

"More wine?" he asked, already reaching for the bottle. "There's not much more than a swallow left."

I held out my glass, watching as the last of the wine trickled in, deep red and promising. "I'll take it. I'm already kinda..."

I paused, searching for the right word as the warmth of the wine mingled with the heat of his proximity.

"Loose?" he suggested, a smile playing at his lips.

"Something like that."

Thunder rumbled again, the sound reverberating through the building and startling us both. His arm dropped from the couch to my shoulders, anchoring me against him.

"Still going," he murmured, his thumb tracing small circles on my shoulder through the cotton of his t-shirt. "Guess you're stuck here a while longer."

"Guess so." I let my head rest against his shoulder, breathing in the subtle scent of him. "Though you did promise me a proper slumber party, and so far all I've gotten is the wine-drunk version of TV show quotes and fancy snacks."

"Well, I hate to disappoint." His voice had dropped lower, taking on a hoarse, husky quality. "What else did you have in mind?"

The wine had made me bold. Or maybe it was the way he looked at me like I was the most fascinating thing in his apartment, or how his voice had gotten lower and softer as the night went on, wrapping around me like velvet.

"Mmmm..." I traced the rim of my wineglass with one finger, meeting his eyes with a playful smile. "We could play another game. By the way, I think I won our game earlier."

"You might have. I honestly stopped counting; I was taking you to lunch no matter who won." Sterling raised an eyebrow, the gesture equally playful and scorching. "What kind of game did you have in mind?"

"How about... Two Truths and a Lie? We could learn some surprising facts about each other."

"I'm game. But let's raise the stakes. Loser of each round has to take a drink."

"You are on." I scooted back into the couch cushions, angling my body toward his. "You go first."

Sterling took a thoughtful sip of wine, his throat working in a way that should not have turned me on... but did. "Okay. I once went skydiving on a dare. I have a black belt in karate. I'm allergic to peanuts."

I studied his face intently, looking for any hint of deception. All three sounded plausible for a man like Sterling—adventurous, athletic, deep, but also playful. But the way his lips twitched made me pause, a tell so subtle I might have missed it if I hadn't been watching him so closely.

"The lie is... the peanut allergy," I declared finally. "You'd have passed up those chocolate peanut butter cups in the snack basket otherwise."

Sterling grinned, lifting his glass in a salute that made the remaining wine catch the light like liquid rubies. "Well played. I do love a good Reese's cup. Your turn."

I took a moment to consider my options, acutely aware of his eyes on me. I wrapped my arms around my knees while I considered my truths. "Alright. I once won a hula hooping contest in college. I have a tattoo of a snake. I'm a secret Trekkie."

He leaned closer, his gaze intense as if trying to read the truth in my eyes. "I'm going to say the lie is the tattoo. You don't strike me as an ink kind of girl."

"Wrong!" I crowed triumphantly, feeling a surge of satisfaction. "I am most definitely not a Trekkie. Star Wars all the way."

"Wait... where is your ink?"

"Wouldn't you like to know?" I smirked, then grabbed his wine glass. "Drink!"

Sterling obliged, taking a healthy swallow of wine, then set his glass back down with an air of determination. "Okay, round two. Gotta get back on my game."

We continued like that, the game becoming progressively sillier and the truths more outlandish as the wine disappeared and our inhibitions lowered. I learned that Sterling spoke passable Spanish, had a childhood fear of clowns, and once got lost in the Paris catacombs on a dare.

In turn, I admitted to teaching myself how to code video games, possessing a collection of vintage comic books that I kept pristine in plastic sleeves, and a brief stint as a competitive mathlete in high school.

Sterling's eyebrows rose in intrigued surprise. "A mathlete? See—beauty and brains is a deadly combo."

I ducked my head, feeling a pleased flush wash across my cheeks at his praise. "I was also president of the robotics club. I was always a huge hit at the science fair. Not so much with the boys, but... tough breaks."

"I bet you were the coolest nerd. Where does a mathlete who builds robots go to school? MIT?"

"I was the coolest nerd at Georgia Tech," I corrected primly.

"My bad. I should've known, Georgia girl." He tipped his glass to me, his eyes never leaving mine. "To the most impressive woman I've met in a very long time."

I clinked my glass against his. "Flattery will get you everywhere, Mr. Carter."

"Oh, I'm counting on it, Ms. Richardson." His eyes held mine, smoldering with open intent. "Okay... circle of truth, right?" He leaned in, voice dropping conspiratorially. "Don't tell anyone but.. Sed and I may have dabbled in a little Dungeons and Dragons back in the day."

I gasped, my eyes wide in delight. "Okay, that settles it. We're having a game night soon."

At some point, Sterling had pulled a throw blanket off the back of the couch, draping it over both our laps as the temperature dropped. When he spoke again, his voice was low and intimate, wrapping around me like silk.

"Can I go again?"

"Sure."

"Okay," he said. "I've never felt this kind of connection with anyone so quickly before. I don't want to make you uncomfortable, but I find you incredibly attractive. And..."

He landed a hand on my thigh and slid higher, his thumb grazing in a slow, teasing circle. "I really, really want to kiss you right now."

"Uhm..." My heart thundered against my ribs, electric and wild in anticipation of what was coming next. "None of those sound like a lie to me. At least I hope they're not."

"They're not." He reached up to tuck a stray curl behind my ear, his fingers trailing along my cheek and down to tip my chin up. The touch was feather-light but sent shock waves down my back. "So... kinda leaving it up to you. I'm happy to move back, get back to watching our show, but I thought I'd just... see if you had any desire to make one of those truths a reality."

In answer, I leaned in, closing the scant distance between us to press my lips to his. He responded immediately, his mouth moving against mine with a hungry urgency that told me he'd been thinking about this—and hoping for it just as much as I had.

One kiss became two, then three, each deeper and more heated than the last. Hands roamed, eager to explore as we shifted on the couch. Sterling pressed me back against the cushions until I was fully reclined beneath him and savoring the weight of him on top of me. I slid my fingers down his back to trace the firm muscles rippling through his shirt.

He kissed a trail along my jaw and down my neck, nipping gently at the sensitive skin, then soothing it with his tongue. A moan rolled from my lips. I felt his answering groan vibrate against my throat.

"The sounds you make... I need more of them."

My only response was to pull him closer, losing myself in the taste and feel of him. The kiss deepened and our bodies melded together. I hadn't felt so safe, so wanted in such a long time.

"Sterling," I gasped as his hands slid under the shirt to caress the bare skin at my waist. "I... I..."

"What can I do for you, Opal?" he murmured against my lips. "Tell me what you need."

My words were lost as he nipped at my earlobe, sending a jolt of pleasure straight to my core. I arched against him and he groaned, his fingers tightening their grip on me.

"I want... I want to have sex with you," I finally managed to say, my skin flush.

His eyes met mine, dark with desire but also searching, making sure I was sure. In them, I saw everything I was feeling reflected back at me. The want, the connection, the sense that this was somehow important. Meant to be.

I held his gaze steadily, letting him see the certainty there. With a growl he stood, pulling me up with him, then grabbed my hand to lead me to his bedroom, kicking the door closed behind us.

Sterling's bedroom was cozy and inviting, with low lighting and plush bedding. He turned to face me, holding my hands in his.

"I need to make sure this is what you really want," he said.

I nodded in breathless anticipation. "Yes. I want this. With you."

Sterling smiled, his eyes softening with tenderness. "Then I want it too," he said, pulling me close for another kiss as we climbed onto the bed. This kiss was slow and exploratory, as if we were trying to savor every minute, every second. His hands were everywhere, roaming over my back and down to my hips. I melted into him, losing myself in the moment.

He pulled away slightly to pull off his shirt, revealing a chiseled chest. My fingers trembled as I reached out to trace the lines of his muscles.

He pulled my shirt up to reveal a lacy bra and overfull cups. The bra had been perfect for the dress I'd worn to dinner but was a bit much underneath a t-shirt.

"Mmmm," he moaned, taking in the view.

"You like?"

"Honey, I am a man. Of course, I like, but... you are stunning."

His fingers toyed with the clasp of the bra until it fell away and joined our discarded clothing on the floor. My breasts dropped, the nipples stiffening in the cool air. His mouth descended on one breast, sucking gently on the hardened nipple while his fingers worked its magic on the other. Pleasure shot through me like a bolt of lightning and I let out a moan that spurred him on.

He continued exploring every inch of me with his hands and mouth until I was squirming, craving more than just kisses and caresses.

"Sterling... please..." I begged. "Don't tease me. It's been too long. We're too close... I need..."

"I've got you," Sterling promised before moving between my legs where I needed him most. He kissed along my inner thighs, teasing before finally giving me what I needed—his tongue against my most sensitive spot.

The pleasure was overwhelming. I fisted the light duvet, gripping tightly as sensations rocked my body. Sterling's mouth and fingers worked in perfect rhythm. I let out a breathless moan, trembling in response to an unrelenting assault.

"Fuckfuckfuckfuckfuck... oh my God!"

"Feels good to you, huh?"

My back arched off the bed as he expertly brought me close, then pulled back and began the ramp up all over again.

"Don't stop!" I gripped his hands when I felt him pulling back. "Please, please, please... don't stop..."

"Not yet," he whispered against my skin. "I want to be inside you when you come. I want to come with you."

He kissed his way back up my body until his lips met mine again. This time it was different—rougher, more intense. His hands gripped my hips, pulling me against him as he deepened the kiss.

I felt him press into me and all coherent thought left my mind as pure instinct took over.

I arched my back, my breath coming in short, sharp gasps as the tension built. Sterling's hands gripped mine, holding them above my head as he thrust deep, then deeper; pounded hard, then faster. I felt as if I was coiled high and tight—a spring ready to snap.

His lips found my neck, kissing and nipping as he whispered encouragement.

"That's it, baby. Just like that... come get it. Take it. It's yours."

We moved together like we'd been made for this, our bodies aligning in perfect sync. Every thrust, every sigh, every grunt and whispered curse wove us closer together until it felt like there was no line between where I ended and he began.

"You about to come?" He rasped. "Let it go if you want to. I'm right behind you."

"Sterling," I gasped, clinging to him as I came undone, the orgasm rippling through me in waves of pure, unadulterated erotic pleasure.

"Yeah, yeah, yeah, yeah!" He groaned, pushing deep,

writing against me as his release pulsed through him. "*Mmmmmmm...* shit!"

After one last thrust, Sterling collapsed on top of me, his weight a comforting pressure as we both struggled to catch our breath. We lay there for a long moment, our chests heaving, our hearts pounding as one.

Finally, he lifted his head. "Opal," he murmured, his voice raw and filled with emotion. "I don't know what just happened, but... I feel like I've known you my whole life."

I stared into Sterling's eyes, trying to find the words to express what I was feeling. But in that moment, words failed me.

I lay there, my body still recovering from an onslaught of pleasure as Sterling's words sank in. The intensity of what we'd just shared, not just physically, but emotionally, was overwhelming.

I was... sated. Deliriously tired. A bit tipsy.

Exposed. Vulnerable.

Terrified.

Chapter Eight

S terling

I let myself in the side door at Sedrick and Blair's house. To the left, the sultry sounds of Jill Scott poured from the speakers in the kitchen where Blair was tearing it up, as far as I could tell. The scent of bacon, grits, and cinnamon rolls made me ravenous.

I turned to the right to Sedrick's home office, where sunlight filtered through blinds, casting striped shadows across the hardwood floor. A few shots of prestigious properties were framed and hung along the walls, flanking a meticulously organized whiteboard.

Sedrick was at his desk surrounded by a neat stack of printed pages. He'd turned a spare bedroom into what he called his "war room," complete with a calendar covered in his cramped handwriting and a trio of monitors. A coffee cup sat at his right elbow, evidence that he'd been at it for hours already. His fingers tapped a steady rhythm on the keyboard, pausing only momentarily as I entered.

"Must be hungry, single man," he said without looking up from his laptop. His fingers continued their precise dance across the keys. "Blair's making a double batch of rolls since Ma called and said she's stopping by after church."

I dropped into one of the club chairs across from his desk, the leather creaking beneath my weight. The chair was well-worn, molded by years of family conversations and late-night strategy sessions. "I thought Ma wasn't speaking to you after you sold the Tiller house to those developers."

Sed sucked his teeth, finally pausing his typing. He swiveled in his chair, the wheels squeaking. "She came around once she saw what they did with it. You know how she gets about preserving the neighborhood's character, but that house has just been sitting next door since Mr. Tiller died. After they went through and restored all of the historic details, she couldn't stop raving about what a good job they did."

He leaned back, rolling his shoulders to stretch. "Besides, I put a chunk of the profit into some new acquisitions for Kindred. The gallery's spring exhibition opens next month. Make sure it's on your calendar."

I nodded, making a note. "That's how you get on her good side? Spend money on the gallery?"

"Apparently. Pop said she's been working harder since she retired than she worked when she was employed."

I picked up one of the property listings on his desk, scanning the details. "This the condo you've been trying to sell me on?"

"No. That's a listing about to go up in Grant Park." He snatched the pages from my fingers, holding it aloft. "But

Sterling doesn't want to look at a house, even though it might be perfect for him."

I wiggled my fingers, asking for it back without asking. He handed it to me. "Three bedrooms, two and a half baths, finished basement, two car garage, nice yard. There's an HOA, which sucks but the fees seem reasonable. Check it out."

"I'm not in the market for a house, but..." I twisted my lips to the side as my eyes skipped down the listing. The house actually appealed to me, was priced to move, and so what if I had a lot of house for a single man? I would have some room to grow, right?

"Let me know. It's going up on Wednesday."

"For sure."

"So...when do I get to know about what you had going on Friday night?" His eyes locked onto mine, sharp and interested. "You ignored my calls all weekend and you got that 'I met somebody' air about you today."

"Man..." A smile hit my face before I could stop it.

Sedrick's eyes widened as he pointed and laughed. "*Yooooo!* Is that your 'I did somebody' face?" He leaned forward, elbows landing precisely on the desk's edge. "It is! Who is she? Lay it out."

"Nothing to lay out." I studied the listing in my hands, but the words blurred together.

"Nothing to lay—brother, please. I know that slap ass grin and don't tell me it's work. That's not your 'I just closed a deal' face."

"I don't have that many faces, Sedrick."

"Talk, Sterling. Or I'll mention it to Ma and Pop and you do not want that."

I sighed, weighing how much to share. Sedrick would

drag it out of me eventually. He always did. "I met someone. From my building."

"The Avian? Hold up—you doin' somebody you gotta see everyday?"

"Do you want to hear about this or not?"

He grabbed his coffee mug, then leaned back in his chair and propped both feet up on the corner of the desk. "I'm sat and ready for story time. What's her name?"

"Opal Richardson."

"Opal Richardson." He tested the name. "Okay, I see you, son. So what's her deal? What's she looking like?"

"You know my type—cute from the front. Even cuter from the back. Brown-skin, natural hair, juicy lips...juicy everything else. Anyway, she works in tech. Wears these big, thick black framed glasses—sexy as fuck on her. Her company has a co-working space a few floors down from the space I'm working in."

"Uh huh." Sedrick was nodding. "Go on..."

"So... I saw her and her friend having lunch Wednesday —after I pissed her off Tuesday morning by taking too long to order coffee, so I bought her lunch Tuesday afternoon."

"Smooth."

"I met her friend, who comes to the building a lot, I guess, because she was all *who is you?* She starts talking about this dinner she's having on Friday, and Opal doesn't have a date and do I want to accompany her to dinner at Marcel—"

"Marcel? *Sheeeeeiiiiiittt!*" Sedrick's whistle carried across the room. "Blair is never allowed to suggest Marcel. Brother, that's not a first date spot. That's a 'meet the parents' spot. That's a 'put a ring on it' spot."

"It wasn't a date." I set the listing down, giving up the pretense of reading it. "Opal's best friend's boyfriend planned to propose. She needed backup to avoid getting set up with someone else. I happened to walk up as they were talking about it and...got hit with an invite."

"Okay, so...." Sedrick kicked his legs off of the desk and sat up. "You had dinner with a fly shorty you met at work at Marcel. On Valentine's Day. As this woman's fake date. To save her from another fake date."

"It wasn't quite like that. She just needed some moral support as the only single person in a group of couples."

"At Marcel. On Valentine's Day."

"I didn't pick the restaurant, man." I threw up my hands in frustration. "And the happy couple picked up the tab. It's not like your pity offer to sit here with Shaw all night was a better plan."

"I'm just trying to wrap my head around this situation." He leaned back again, sipping coffee from his mug. "So did you even go to dinner? Blair canceled our Garden Room reservations 'cause that storm was moving in. No grass wall Instagram photos for me."

"Had a good ass salad, ribeye steak, lobster bisque, red wine, champagne, some chocolate thing. Opal was lookin' fine in this crepe-like black dress. Had everything sittin'... *nice*. Right after the proposal, the storm blew through like a monster. She didn't feel like she could drive home so..."

I fought the smile that wanted to spread by pressing my lips together but it didn't work. "She stayed at my place."

"And... nothing happened right? An innocent little sleepover? A slumber party if you will..."

I shook my head, frowning. "I ain't say all that."

"You sly dog!" Sedrick slapped his desk hard enough to rattle his monitors, his laughter bouncing off the walls. "That explains why you're in here looking like you discovered electricity."

"What does that even mean, Sedrick?"

"I don't know, some shit Pop says. Your face is telling on you right now, though." He settled back in his chair, still grinning. "Go 'head. Get to the good part."

"We talked all night." I found myself wanting to explain, to make him understand this wasn't just some random hookup. "She's brilliant, Sed. She's developing this platform for diversity initiatives in tech. The way she talks about it... it's like... her life's work. She's passionate about making real change happen."

"Uh huh. And..."

"And...she's funny. Sharp. We watched A Different World until three AM, just quoting lines and our favorite episodes. She told me about this YouTube channel that's breaking down all the episodes. Also she's...nerdy. Like high school mathlete nerdy. Robotics Club nerdy."

The smug grin dropped from Sedrick's face and he sat up, coming close. "D&D nerdy?" He asked, almost in a whisper.

I nodded. "For sure."

"Shit!" He slammed the desk and slid back in the chair. "Have you proposed yet, little brother? Fine, sexy, smart, *and* a blerd? Lock it down!"

"I don't know about all that. I just... you know... we had a good time. I'd like to have more good times if she's open to it."

"Yeah, I feel that," Sedrick said. "You know who you sound like right now? Me when I first met Blair. All stupid happy, can't keep that grin off your face when you talk about her."

"It's not... I mean..." I scrubbed my face as if I could erase the expression that seemed permanently imprinted on my features. "I don't know what it is yet. But it feels different."

"Different like..."

The question made me pause. How could I explain the instant connection, the way conversation flowed effortlessly, the feeling that I'd known her far longer than a few days?

"Like meeting someone and knowing immediately they matter to you." I stared at the ceiling, choosing my words carefully. "We talked about everything and nothing. She gets my nerdy jokes—she definitely doesn't just laugh to be polite. She calls out bullshit in this refreshingly direct way. No games, no pretense."

"Sounds like exactly what you need." Sedrick's teasing tone shifted into something more serious. "You've been all about the grind since that mess with your old firm. When's the last time you actually got excited about someone like this?"

"Kenya—"

"Absolutely does not count. You liked her for what... three months? Then spent the next six months avoiding her."

"She wanted to move in after two weeks, Sed. Opal is nothing like Kenya."

"Clearly," Sedrick said. "So when's the next date?"

I hesitated, fiddling with the cuff of my shirt. "We... haven't exactly made plans yet." I pulled out my phone to check it. The text exchange between Opal and me remained stubbornly blank, just like it had since Saturday morning when I woke up and she was gone. She'd left a note to thank me for my hospitality and that she would see me around the building. "I texted her to say hey on Saturday night. Again this morning— she won a bet and I'm supposed to take her to lunch. No response."

"Hmm." His smile faded into a frown. "Maybe she's busy?"

"Maybe. She's close to launch on her platform and she works long hours." I kept my voice steady despite the concern creeping in. "I'm not gonna blow her up, but..."

"But you're worried."

"I just wanted to check in. Make sure she knows I don't consider anything that happened between us to be a one-off."

"Sterling... man, listen. Sometimes women get in their heads about moving fast. Especially if they didn't plan on moving fast. Especially on the first date— and I know it wasn't a date, but let's call a spade a spade. She might need time to settle into whatever is happening."

"You think?" The way hope bloomed in my chest was almost embarrassing, but it made me a little lighter. "She mentioned her last relationship ended badly. Her ex stole her app idea and launched it without her. Made a fortune off her work."

"That's foul as hell. Some people really ain't shit. So that means she ain't about trusting nobody new. Getting burned like that changes how you move."

I remembered how Opal tensed when she talked about her ex, pain still evident in her eyes years later. "I don't want her thinking this was casual for me. It wasn't about..." I trailed off, not sure how to finish that sentence.

"It wasn't about getting laid," he finished for me. "I get it. Look, give her some space. A couple days, maybe. Then reach out again. Let her know you enjoyed spending time with her and you'd like to see her again, but no pressure. If she got hurt before, she needs to be in the driver's seat. Especially if things moved fast."

"But what if—"

"If it's real, she'll hit you back." His voice carried that big brother tone I remembered from childhood. "And if she doesn't, her loss. But you sitting here checking your phone every five seconds isn't gonna make her text any faster."

I pushed out a sigh, knowing Sedrick was right. I needed to give Opal some space and respect her boundaries. But the thought of her not wanting to see me again made my stomach churn.

"I appreciate you, man," I said, grateful for Sedrick's wisdom. "I'll take your advice and give her some time. When did you get so wise about this stuff?"

"You just told me the other day I used to be a ladies' man. A real loverboy."

"Yeah, but... for real..."

"For real? Being married to a smart woman. You think that happened by accident?" He gestured at the wall of family photos behind his desk. "Every good thing I've got came from learning when to push and when to let things breathe. You gotta trust the process."

"Trust the process?" I laughed. "You sound like a life coach."

"Maybe I missed my calling," Sedrick chuckled. "I stole that from Shaw's coach. He's always telling the boys about how practice pays off. By the way, you missed his last game. Boy's a beast."

"I saw the clip Pop sent. That reverse layup in the third quarter was cold."

"Yeah, that's going on his highlight reel. Georgia Tech's already making noise. Blair's worried he'll go too far away for college."

"Tech's a good program. Strong academics too."

"That's what I keep telling her. Fingers crossed he wants to stay close, but I won't be upset if he goes to a school where the NBA can see him." Sedrick's phone buzzed. He glanced at it and grinned. "My better half says breakfast is ready. And Ma just pulled up."

As we walked toward the kitchen, Sedrick gripped my shoulder. "For what it's worth, it's nice to see your nose open about somebody. Just... fair warning, this woman has you looking real happy, and Ma is gonna catch on. You better think about something real sad and serious. Wipe that pussy off your face."

Blair looked up from the oven, her eyes moving between us. "Wipe what off his face? Why do I feel like I missed something good?"

"Because your brother-in-law is in *loooove*," Sedrick announced, dropping into his seat at the kitchen island.

"I am not in love." Even I heard how weak that sounded. "And I am not discussing this shit in front of my mother. Dead it, or I'll never share another thing."

Blair's eyes lit up as she set a pan of cinnamon rolls on the cooling rack, then planted a hand on her hip. "When Mother Carter leaves, it's on."

Chapter Nine

pal

My thumb hovered over Sterling's latest text. I dared myself to reply.

> Hope you're having a good weekend. Still owe you that lunch.

It was the third message since I'd slipped out of his apartment early Saturday morning, leaving nothing but a hastily scrawled note of thanks. Each text had been casual. He made it plain he wasn't crowding me, but diligently letting me know he was thinking of me without demanding anything in return.

No pressure, just... presence.

The first had come Saturday evening:

> Made it home safe, I hope? The storm
> finally cleared out.

Then Sunday:

> Good morning. Just wanted to say I really
> enjoyed getting to know you Friday night.

And now this one about lunch, reminding me of our silly game at Marcel, of our shared laughter and secret game at that table. Of what came after.

In the end, I couldn't bring myself to respond to any of them.

Even if I hadn't planned to be late to work, I'd have an excuse. The streets were still a mess from Friday night's rager of a storm—trees had fallen, blocking off roads. Water lines and sewer systems were clogged and backed up. It worked out to time my arrival perfectly—late enough to miss the morning rush with little chance of running into Sterling.

Joya looked up from prepping sandwiches for lunch, surprise flickering across her face. "Well, look who finally discovered there are other hours in the morning."

"The commute was pure shit," I replied, setting my bag on the counter. "And I practically had to park on the top floor of the parking deck. I miss Princess Parking on the bottom floor."

Done with my rant, I forced a smile I didn't feel. "Can I get my usual, please?"

"Sure." She started on my drink, but I felt her eyes on me. "You feeling okay? Not like you to come in late."

"Mmhmm. I'm good," I replied, maybe too quickly.

"If you say so." She handed over my americano with a

look that made me squirm. "Sterling was in earlier asking about you."

I winced internally. I hoped it didn't show on my face. Of course Sterling would notice my absence, both physical and digital. "Oh yeah?"

"He asked if I'd seen you because your office was still dark. He wanted to make sure you were okay. Sweet of him to check."

I tapped my phone on the reader, avoiding her eyes. "I'm alive and well. Thanks, Joya."

Back in my office, I threw myself into work. The Circuit2Soul Gala was less than a week away, and the Align platform demo needed to be perfect. I had mock-ups to review, bugs to squash, and approximately eight million emails demanding immediate attention.

But my mind kept drifting to Friday night. The storm raging outside while we sat cozy on his couch. The wine smoothing the path as we traded truths and lies. Sterling's clothes that made my hamper smell like him—and made me not want to wash them so the scent would never leave my nose. The way he'd looked at me like I was fascinating, like he wanted to memorize every detail.

The sensation of his hands on my skin...

"Focus!" I hissed at myself, shaking my head to clear it. I pulled up the latest bug report, determined to lose myself in work.

Cannot replicate error in test environment. User reports inconsistent behavior when...

His hands sliding under my shirt, teasing and tempting...

System timeout occurring at random intervals...

The taste of wine on his lips and the probe of his tongue as he explored my mouth... and everywhere else...

Front-end elements fail to load properly in Safari browser...

The way his voice had seemed ragged and tattered when he came, and the way he didn't hold back...

"Damn it!" I slammed my laptop closed, pressing the heels of my hands against my eyes until I saw stars.

This was exactly why I couldn't get involved with anyone. My reputation, my career trajectory, everything I'd worked for depended on the next month. ConnecTech would get this one chance to make an impact—who knew what the future held for Diversity, Equity and Inclusion policies?

I could not fuck this up. I couldn't afford distractions. Especially not tall, handsome distractions with gentle hands and gorgeous smiles who looked at me like I was someone important to him.

My phone lit up with Asia's FaceTime request. I almost ignored it, but she'd been blowing up my texts all morning. Better to face her now than let her show up at my office.

"Finally!" Asia's face filled my screen, wearing the happy glow of a newly engaged woman. I caught a glimpse of her home office behind her. "I've been trying to reach you since seven AM! I had to watch that green dot on Messenger mock me while you ignored three of my calls."

I slumped back in my chair, rubbing my temples. Three unread messages from Asia glared at me from my phone. I'd been avoiding everyone this morning, not just Sterling.

"Sorry. I've been in back-to-back meetings."

"Lies." She leaned closer to her camera, eyes narrowing. "Have you texted Sterling back? Or did you just leave him on read? After the night you had?"

I huffed. "Who told you he's been texting?"

"You did! Saturday when you called me freaking out. And Sunday when you were still freaking out."

She waved a hand around. I caught a glimpse of her engagement ring sparkling. "I thought the sex was mind-blowing? Life-changing? I thought you said he was trying to fuck the anxiety right out of your body?"

"Oh my God." Heat crept up my neck as I remembered frantically calling Asia on Saturday while sitting in my cold car in Sterling's parking garage.

"I fucked up. Bad." The whole night tumbled out of my mouth before she could even say hello. "I mean... I didn't fuck up, it was good. So good...but I shouldn't have. I told him shit nobody else knows. We talked about everything—D&D and old TV shows and he just gets it, he gets me, and I..."

I sucked in a sharp breath, hearing how unhinged I sounded. "I let my guard down. All the way down. What the hell is wrong with me?"

"Breathe, honey." Asia's voice was steady, grounding. "Take a long breath, then let it out."

"And now I can't stop thinking about him," I said, refusing to follow her orders to breathe. "Like how he listened—really listened when I talked about work. Or how he made me laugh about Whitley and Dwayne until my sides hurt. What...what do I do with all of that?"

She'd talked me down from my panic, listened as I cycled between wanting to run back to him and wanting to change my name and move to another state. When his first text came that evening, I screenshot it and sent it to her immediately.

She'd replied:

He's checking on you. That's sweet.

But sweet was dangerous. Sweet made me want things I couldn't want right now.

"I cannot believe I said all that out loud," I muttered, coming back to the present moment. My face felt hot enough to fry an egg. "I must have been dickmatized."

"And that's bad because...?" Asia prodded gently.

"I don't have time for this shit right now! I need to focus on work."

Asia chuckled, but it wasn't a cheery, friendly sound. "That's so much bullshit and you know it." Her voice softened. "Opal...friend...I'm going to virtually hold your hand when I tell you this: what Kellan did was awful. He betrayed your trust in the worst way. But Sterling isn't Kellan."

"I know that."

"Do you? Because it seems like you're punishing Sterling for something he didn't do." She paused, then added quietly, "And punishing yourself in the process."

I stared at my reflection in the FaceTime screen, barely recognizing the woman looking back at me. When had I become this person? Was I like this when I met Kellan?

No, I told myself. I immediately knew that I was soft and open and trusting. I just knew I'd found The One. And that was the problem. I was too soft and too open and too trusting and Kellan took full advantage.

"I can't go through that again, Asia. I can't fall for someone and then discover it was all a lie."

"Baby girl, that's exactly what Kellan wanted—to make you afraid to trust anyone else. To make you doubt yourself so much you'd never see how trash he really was. Sterling is a good man, Opal," she quoted from one of our favorite movies, Waiting to Exhale. "Maybe give him a chance to prove it?"

"And if I'm wrong? If I'm just seeing what I want to see?"

"And if you're right to give him more than five days to show himself to be a good dude?" She countered. "What if this is your chance at something real and you're too scared to take it? What if you spend the rest of your life wondering what could have been because you were too afraid to find out?"

"I..." My voice caught in my throat. I cleared it and tried again. "I don't know how to do this anymore, Asia. I don't know how to trust my judgment anymore."

"Then trust mine. Trust that I wouldn't be pushing this if I didn't think he was worth it." A gentle, sympathetic smile bent her lips. "You deserve to be happy, Opal. You deserve someone who sees your worth and celebrates it. Someone who makes you feel safe enough to be vulnerable."

"But what if—"

"No more what ifs! Girl, I swear..."

She threw up her hands in exasperation, turned her chair around, then turned it back.

"You know what? Fine. Ghost him. Push away the first man who's made you smile—really smile—in years. Keep living in that apartment you hate because you're too scared to make a change. Pour everything into work until you burn out and ConnecTech tosses you out for someone just as brilliant but younger and cheaper. But don't come crying to me when you're sixty and alone with nothing but your debugged code to keep you warm at night."

"That's not fair—"

"Neither is what you're doing to Sterling. Or to yourself. You just told me that he sees you and hears you and he gets you. When's the last time anyone that wasn't me did that for you?"

Before I could respond, a notification popped up on my calendar. I wiped my eyes and snapped a tissue from the box on my desk. "Shit, I have a meeting in ten and I have to present. I have to go."

"Think about what I said!" Asia called out. "And text that man back before he gives up on you!"

I ended the call and dropped my head onto my desk with a thunk. Asia's words kept echoing in my head. What if this was my chance at something real? What if I was letting fear rob me of happiness?

What if, what if, what if... what if there were no more what-ifs?

By late afternoon, my eyes were burning from staring at screens and my neck ached from tension. I'd missed lunch again, too caught up in trying to fix a stubborn UI bug that kept appearing in our latest test build. The platform was stable overall, but something still felt off in the interface. I couldn't put my finger on what was wrong, but I knew it wasn't ready for the gala demo.

A knock at my door startled me out of a trance. Through the frosted glass, I recognized Sterling's silhouette.

My heart stopped. Then raced double-time.

I pushed back from my desk, smoothing my blouse as I crossed to the door. My hand hesitated on the handle for just a moment before I pulled it open.

Sterling stood there in dark jeans and a crisp button-down that stretched across his shoulders, sleeves rolled to expose his forearms. He held two cups—and I knew without asking one was my usual from Coffee Theory.

"Hi," he said simply, his eyes finding mine. No condemnation, but also no spark. "Can we talk?"

"Uhm...I'm actually in the middle of something." I gestured at my screens, my eyes not meeting his. "The platform demo—"

"I know you stay busy." He stayed in the doorway, holding out one of the coffee cups. "But everyone needs a break sometimes."

The gesture hit me right in the chest. I stared at the cup, fighting the urge to smile. "Sterling..."

"Five minutes? That's all I'm asking."

I glanced at my desk by the window, then at the small seating area in the front of my office. The couch and chairs were angled away from both the door and the windows, offering at least some privacy.

"Fine. Five minutes." I stepped back, letting him enter. "We can sit over here."

Sterling followed me to the lounge area, settling into one of the chairs while I took the corner of the couch. He set my coffee on the small table between us, close enough for me to reach but not forcing me to take it.

"You've been avoiding me," he said simply. No accusation in his tone, just quiet certainty.

"I've been working." The lie felt wrong coming out of my mouth but it was the best I had to offer. "I can't allow distractions to—"

"Is that what I am? A distraction?"

I wrapped my arms around myself, hating how vulnerable I felt. "You know it's more complicated than that."

"I know something happened between us Friday night," he said, when I didn't respond. "I felt it. You felt it too."

"Sterling, I can't do this right now."

"Can't? Or won't?" He picked up his coffee, took a slow sip. "Because I've been replaying every moment of that night, trying to figure out where I could have gone wrong—"

"You didn't do anything wrong." The words burst out before I could stop them. "That's... that's not what this is about."

"Then help me understand, because right now all I know is I shared an unprecedented connection with someone, and instead of talking about it, or at least staying for frozen waffles and a couple episodes of a show we both like...she disappeared. Left me a note like I was some random hookup. Left me on read like I'm the problem."

The hurt in his voice made my chest ache. "I didn't mean to make you feel that way."

"How did you mean for me to feel?" When I didn't answer, he sighed. "I understand more than you think I understand. You've been burned before. Bad. Old dude took advantage of your trust."

I stiffened. "You don't know anything about—"

"I know enough." He set his coffee down, his movements deliberate as he leaned forward. "I know you guard yourself carefully. I know your work means everything to you. I know you use it as a barrier. And I know someone used that against you once."

"How did you—"

"Because I see you, Opal. I see how your mind works, how you see everything in code. Remember analyzing the dinner table? That's a you thing. I see how hard you work to keep people at a distance while pretending you're focused. And I see how scared you are right now, because what happened between us wasn't just physical. It meant something."

Tears pricked at my eyes. I blinked them back furiously. "It can't mean something. It was a few hours compared to... a lifetime. I can't... I can't do this again. Not now. Not with everything—"

"I'm not asking for everything." He moved next to me, close enough that I could see the flecks of amber in his eyes that I had never noticed before. "I'm asking for one thing—to show you that not everyone will take advantage of your trust. That maybe something real is worth the risk."

For a moment, I wavered. It would be so easy to lean in, to let myself believe.

But then I remembered Kellan's sincerity. How genuine he'd seemed right up until the moment he betrayed me.

I stood abruptly, needing distance. "I have a lot of work to do. I have to have the platform ready to demonstrate on Saturday at this... huge tech industry event. I cannot risk fucking it up. And... and the launch is in three weeks. I need...I need..."

"Space?" Sterling stood too, but didn't move closer. "I'll give you space. But I want you to know something." He waited until I met his eyes. "I'm not him, Opal. And I'm not going anywhere. When you're ready to talk—really talk—I'll be here."

He turned to leave, then paused at the door. "Your coffee's getting cold."

* * *

Much later that evening, I pulled into the driveway of a two-story modern farmhouse in Decatur. The motion-sensor lights flickered on, casting a glow over the carefully maintained landscaping. My mother's touch was evident in every precisely trimmed hedge and strategically planted flower bed.

I dropped my messenger bag onto the little side table by the kitchen entrance, the same spot I'd been dropping my bags since middle school. The leather slumped against the wall, heavy with the day's accumulated stress.

I kicked off my shoes and padded into the kitchen.

"Hi, Mom. Smells so good in here. I missed lunch."

She was in motion, her movements a choreographed dance between the stove and the counter. Steam rose from a pot, the scent of rosemary and lemon filling the kitchen. Grilled artichokes sizzled on a platter, edges perfectly charred, promising that particular magic she worked with the simplest ingredients.

"You're late, love," she said without turning around. "Everything alright?"

I exhaled as I sat at the island, feeling the weight of the day shuffle off of my shoulders the way it only did when I sat at my mother's table. "Long day. Traffic was a mess. People always forget how to drive when I'm in a hurry."

The house breathed around me—a living museum of our family history. Photos lined the walls like a carefully curated exhibit: my parents' wedding day, my graduation from Georgia Tech, my father in his white coat, my mother in academic regalia. Each image was a testament to hard-won victories, to education as both weapon and wings.

Copper pots my father had brought back from a medical conference in Brazil hung above the stove. A hand-carved wooden spoon from my mother's family in Georgia rested in a ceramic holder. Every object told a story of migration, of survival, of Black excellence carved out inch by hard-won inch.

Mom glanced over her shoulder, those sharp eyes taking me in. "You look like you're carrying the entire tech industry on those shoulders."

I managed a weak laugh, rolling my arms forward, then back. "I feel like I am, too."

Mom turned from the stove, wooden spoon in hand. "Well, your father's very excited for the gala. He's been bragging to everyone at the hospital that his daughter is presenting her invention to the whole city."

I groaned. "Oh, God. Where is he, by the way?"

"He had a last-minute patient drop by. He said to start without him. Dr. Richardson is about to show off his tech genius progeny to every person who will stop to listen."

The image was both mortifying and adorable. My father, respected physician, never missed an opportunity to talk about my work, even when it wasn't really worth talking about. "He's going to have a whole speech prepared, isn't he?"

"You know it," she confirmed, sliding an artichoke onto a plate. "Complete with quotes about how your platform is going to revolutionize hiring."

I picked up my fork, feeling my sullen mood pass like a dark cloud, revealing a sudden hunger. "It's not just about hiring, though. It's about creating a lasting change. Measuring not just who gets in the door, but who advances. Who stays. Who feels supported."

She settled into a chair next to me, her movements deliberate. The way she listened, made space for me and my opinions, thoughts, and emotions had always been an art form. Complete attention, no interruption, creating space for the full complexity of my developing brain.

"I haven't heard about the progress of the platform. Talk to me," she said. Not a request. An invitation.

While we ate, I talked about the feature that tracked micro-aggressions through anonymized reporting. About how the platform could identify retention patterns that most companies missed. How it wasn't just about metrics, but about creating environments where talent could truly thrive.

Her attention never wavered. She nodded and commented as if it was the most interesting thing she'd ever heard. This was how they'd always been—whether I was talking about a middle school science project or a complex professional breakthrough. Fully present. Fully believing. Fully supporting.

"You know who would just bust with pride right now?" she asked, when I had wound down what would eventually become my speech at the gala. "Your grandmother Layla would have just loved this. She spent her entire career being the first. The only. Always having to prove she belonged. I had some of that, too."

The comment landed with unexpected weight. My grandmother fought for every inch of professional space she'd claimed.

"I'm just trying to stand on her shoulders," I said quietly.

"You are. And you're extending her reach. Mine, too. You're building something that will help countless others stand tall too."

I felt a lump form in my throat. "I hope others see that. There's still so much to do."

"I know how you feel about certain eras in your life, but from my perspective, you have never failed. You've never failed to learn something that pushed you further. You have never failed to let something teach you a lesson. Everything will be alright, love."

We fell into a comfortable silence as we finished our meal. My mind drifted back to Sterling, to how he had dampened the look in his eyes when he'd come to my office. On Friday night, he'd seemed...hopeful and happy. And for a moment, I was too. Then I let something ugly take root in my brain and I hadn't been right since.

"Mom...can I ask you something kind of personal?"

"Mmhmm, of course," she said, not looking up from the last bite of chicken on her plate. "What's on your mind?"

I inhaled a fortifying breath, then pushed out, "How did you know Dad was the one? Like...did you know right away? Did you make him work for your trust? How did it go?"

Slowly she turned her head, giving me the softest smile. "I thought there was something besides work going on in that mind of yours. I didn't figure on it being a man, but... let's see."

She put down her fork and knife, pondering for a long moment, her eyes distant as if looking back through time. "You know, when I met your father, I was so focused on my career. He was a friend of the family and he'd just had his white coat ceremony. Quite handsome. He knew it. He wanted to know if *I* knew it."

I giggled. I'd heard this part of the story often.

"I think I was just open to whatever was going to happen with him. I left it in the Lord's hands and let Vernon know that's where I'd left it. So if he was up to no good, he could deal with the Lord about it. I went about my business, and... what is it the women say? Keep the same energy?"

I nodded.

"Now, Vernon gave 'we're getting married in six months' energy." She paused, rapidly blinking. "I wasn't quite ready for that."

"But you two were married less than a year after you met."

Mom nodded, bobbing her head. "That we were. I had

to search my heart to know if it was okay to let her fall for this man. Was he good? Was he kind? Did I even like him? Did he like me? Do I like me when I am with him? Now, love...I think that was the closer, right there."

"How so?" I asked, twisting to face her.

"It's like when I tell you that your dad might be walking around that gala with a photo of you on a lanyard. That man is so, so proud of you. He's vocal about it, not just to your face but behind your back. He has always been the same man with me. He brags on his wife that teaches at Spelman all the time. It's getting a little silly, but I let him keep going because I like how he makes me feel. I like how I have felt about myself when I am in his presence this whole time we have been married."

"Mommy..." I swiped at a tear that spilled down my cheek. "That's so beautiful. And...it's really helpful."

"I hope so. Now you tell whoever this is that you're putting whatever is going on in the Lord's hands. And he can deal with the man upstairs about it. And also tell him he does not want to deal with Vernon and Constance about it. You hear me?"

I couldn't hold in my laughter. It was like a dam had broken and all the tension I'd been carrying suddenly released. "Yes ma'am," I managed between giggles. "I'll be sure to pass along the message."

As I climbed into my car, I texted Asia.

> Anyway you can play hooky late tomorrow afternoon? I have a wild hair up my ass. I might actually buy something in a color. I need something that says, 'I'm here, and I'm changing everything.'

My phone buzzed. It was too quick for Asia to reply

back, especially at night. As much as she bitched about me ignoring her calls, she could take up to an hour to answer a text.

When I checked my messages, the text was from Sterling.

> Just saying hey. Had a good day. The view from the window said you had a long, rough one. I'm holding off on A Different World episodes so we can watch together. Hope to see you at the cafe in the morning. If not, have an amazing day.

> By the way…that tech event you mentioned…is it Circuit2Soul?

Sterling's message felt like a gentle nudge in the direction my mother had already sent me in. I grabbed the phone from its mount and held the slim device in my hand. My fingers hovered, then I began to type:

> Hey. You up?

I hit send before I could second-guess myself. Asia's response popped up right after that:

> Hallelujah! We're hitting Lenox Square. Be ready for yellow! No arguments.

I groaned. The universe, it seemed, was conspiring to push me out of my comfort zone on every level.

Chapter Ten

S terling

I'd just sunk into the couch, beer in hand, when my phone vibrated with an incoming text. I'd texted Opal, and despite our conversation, expected her to ignore me. It was Sedrick with another funny meme, I figured, so when I picked it up and swiped it open, I almost dropped it when I saw Opal's name at the top of my text message inbox.

> Hey. You up?

I blinked at the message, brain taking a moment to catch up with what I was seeing. After days of radio silence, of convincing myself I'd royally fucked up whatever this thing between us was, she was reaching out.

> I just texted you so…yeah. What's up? You okay?

The typing bubble appeared, three dots blinking in and out of existence. I took a swig of beer, waiting for the dots to stop bouncing.

> Can we talk? In person? I'm on my way to you now if that's alright.

I was off the couch before I'd even finished reading her message, bottle abandoned on the coffee table, headed for the shower.

> Of course. Drive safe.

The forty minutes that followed were some of the longest of my life. I hopped in and out of the shower, slapped some lotion on my skin, brushed my hair, my goatee, and my teeth. When the knock finally came, I practically lunged for the door, swinging it open to reveal Opal standing there.

She was wearing the clothes she'd had on when I had come to her office to talk to her—dark denim jeans and boots, a black cable knit sweater, her hair pulled back into a neat bun. I noticed a set line to her jaw that said she had come to face something head-on. I hoped she hadn't driven all the way to my place to let me down gently.

"Hi," she said. "Thanks for letting me come by so late."

"Yeah, of course." I stepped back, gesturing for her to come in. "I'm just glad to see you."

She moved past me into the apartment, her perfume lingering. I inhaled the musky, floral vanilla, the scent settling into my lungs like a balm. She was standing in the middle of the living room, looking slightly lost. It was such a contrast to the put-together woman I was used to seeing, all sharp lines and quick wit.

She seemed so open and vulnerable. I wanted to hug her, but refrained, shoving my hands in the pockets of the cotton lounge pants I'd put on to keep from reaching for her. "What's going on?"

She inhaled a deep breath, exhaling slowly. When her eyes met mine, there was a new steadiness there, a calm in the center of the storm.

"I owe you an apology," she said, each word carefully chosen. "And an explanation—"

"You don't owe—" I began to protest.

"I do," she countered. "Let me just get it out. The way I left things the other morning, sneaking out on you after you showed me so much hospitality that you didn't have to, then ignoring your messages...that was rude. And unlike me. And it wasn't fair. To you or to me."

"Thank you for the apology. I appreciate it." I kept my tone even, trying not to let the riot of emotions in my chest color my words. "I can't lie, I've been worried I'd done something to push you away. I thought maybe I read this whole situation wrong."

Opal shook her head. "You didn't do anything wrong, Sterling. This is all me. My issues, my baggage. You've been...unbelievable, actually. And that's what's been so hard for me."

She took a step closer, close enough to count the freckles dusting her nose.

"The truth is, I'm a wimp. I'm so scared right now. Of this, of you, of how quickly and intensely I'm falling. Of even admitting I'm falling. It caught me completely off guard and everything in me is screaming to slow down, to stop, don't show emotion, be cool. No man is this nice for long. No man is this amazing for long. He's gonna use you like..."

She stopped, forcing out a shaky breath, then nervously ran a palm over her head and squeezed her bun.

"Opal..." Her name fell from my lips on a sigh. I lifted a hand, slowly, giving her time to pull away. When she didn't, I cupped her cheek, thumb stroking over the smooth skin. "I'm scared too. This shit popped up quick. I might fuck this up. I might be too sure, and act too cocky and move too fast. But if I'm honest? I'm excited to know somebody new. Somebody so...you. I don't connect with people on a personal level the way I have with you."

She leaned into my touch, eyes fluttering closed for a moment. "It's been a long time for me too. And the last time....I've been protecting myself ever since."

I thought of the pain I'd seen in her eyes when she talked about her ex, the way her anger seeped around the edges when she spoke of him. Rage flared in my chest at the thought of someone treating her so callously.

"I hear you. And I'm so sorry you went through that. I understand the impulse and I'm never going to fault you for looking out for you. But Opal..." I ducked my head, catching her eye. "I promise I will do everything in my power not to remind you of him. *Everything.*"

Her smile was small, but it was real. "I know. Deep down, I know you aren't him. It's hard to turn off that voice in my head."

"Maybe I can be louder than that voice. I can say it, and I can just...be that dude that treats you way better. That respects your time and your intellect and your feelings." I reached for her hand, tangling our fingers together. "We can drown out that voice together. We don't have to make a big deal of it right now. Let's take this thing one day at a time, one step at a time. No pressure, no expectations. Just... being together. Letting it go where it's gonna go and not being afraid to let it go there."

Opal squeezed my hand. "I think I'd like that. My mom actually gave me some really good advice. She said to put my trust in God's hands. I took that to mean that I should be brave and have faith, and not punish a good man for another man's sins."

Pride bloomed in me at her words, at the thought that she considered me a good man. That she was willing to take a chance on me, on us.

"Your mom sounds like a wise woman. I'll have to thank her when I meet her."

Opal's brows shot up high, a surprised cackle escaping her. "Meet her? Getting a little ahead of yourself aren't you?"

I grinned, tugging her closer with our joined hands. "I'm just saying. If this goes where I'm hoping it goes, I'll need her on my side."

"You're not wrong about that. She did say to tell you that you do not want to deal with Doctors Vernon and Constance Richardson."

"Doctors? Plural?"

"Dr. Vernon Richardson is a family physician. Dr. Constance Richardson is a professor of Modern African American Literature at Spelman."

I let out a low whistle. "Impressive. And slightly intimidating. But I see where you get your smarts."

Opal shook her head, amused. Then her gaze turned assessing, a playful glint sparking in her eyes as she propped her hands on her hips. "You know, I'm having the strangest sensation of déjà vu. Me showing up at your door in clothes

I can't chill out in, expecting snacks and drinks and conversation..."

I snorted, the remaining tension bleeding out of the room. "I mean...I don't know about you, but I could go for a replay. Minus the storm."

"Hmm..." Opal tapped a finger against her chin, pretending to consider my proposition. Then she moved in close and wrapped her arms around my neck, pressing her body flush against mine. The feel of her body against mine, soft and yielding, left me dizzy. "I could be persuaded," she murmured, her breath fanning across my lips.

I slid my hands around her until she was all the way in my arms. "Say less. We already know where my t-shirts and hoodies are about to end up. Might as well get it started. I'll raid the kitchen and get us set up in the living room."

Opal captured my lips in a light, teasing kiss, bringing a groan from me. I had to physically pull her arms from me, then push her toward my bedroom to dig through my drawers. Not that I would have minded, but I didn't really want to get down in the middle of my living room.

When she emerged a few minutes later, swimming in a sweatshirt and a pair of my workout shorts, I had to take a moment to just...look at her. She'd pulled her hair out of the bun so it was big and puffy. She'd scrubbed her face and taken out her earrings. Opal was gorgeous, all bare feet and soft lines.

She caught me staring and quirked an eyebrow. "What? Too soon to show you the natural me?"

"Not at all, baby. I'm really liking you this way." I shook my head, at a rare loss for words. "You're beautiful."

She ducked her head with a smile, then quickly trotted over to the couch. "Flattery will get you so far, Sterling. So far. Can we start A Different World from the beginning?"

"Yes. Yes to everything."

Opal curled into my side like she'd always belonged there, her head finding that perfect spot on my shoulder. I draped an arm around her, fingers toying with the ends of her hair, and pressed play on the remote.

Phoebe Snow's rendition of the theme song filled the room via surround sound speakers. I felt a deep satisfaction settle inside me. This feeling was everything I wanted—lazy evenings on the couch, early morning coffee dates, inside jokes, shared looks and learning all the little things that made her tick.

I saw the possibility of a future with her in it.

The realization should have scared me, could have made me an immature, ghosting fool. All I felt, though, was a bone-deep certainty, a calm in the center of my soul that said, "there you are, brother. Been waiting for you."

I pressed a kiss to Opal's temple, smiling against her skin when she made a contented little hum. She twisted so her body faced me and draped her legs over my lap. I couldn't stop myself from leaning in and pressing a soft kiss to her lips. It was meant to be quick but turned into something more as Opal opened her mouth.

My hand found its way to the back of her neck as I pulled her closer. "I thought you wanted to watch this show from the beginning," I whispered against the skin of her neck. I couldn't get enough of whatever scent she was wearing.

"I mean...this is the pilot, right?" Opal asked, sitting up. With one hand, she pulled the sweatshirt up and over her head to reveal her breasts, unencumbered by lace and satin. My breathing hitched at the sudden reveal, and I couldn't tear my eyes away from her.

She smirked, clearly enjoying the effect she had on me.

"Uhm...yeah. The pilot. So it's like...not technically the first episode," I managed to say, my eyes transfixed on her dark areolas and hardening nipples. My hands moved of their own accord, pulling her fully onto my lap. She straddled me, grinding down against the growing bulge in my pants.

I responded quickly, directing her movements as she rocked in my lap.

"Fuck," I pushed out, moving one hand to a breast so I could guide her to my mouth and swirl my tongue around the hard nub, alternating between gentle nips and soothing licks.

She shuddered, vocalizing her pleasure with a low moan, holding me close as I lavished attention on one breast, then moved to the other. Her fingers slid down my chest, past the band of my pants and closed around me. I was already hard, pulsing, seeking something warm and wet.

I groaned around the nipple in my mouth as she began to stroke me. I pushed down the shorts she'd just borrowed from me and her panties, baring her slick core to the cool air. My fingers found her clit and started to rub in slow circles, in rhythm to her strokes.

"Mmmmm," she hummed, her head tossed back. "Yes... just like that.."

Her hips rocked against my hand, seeking more friction. I obliged, slipping two fingers inside her while my thumb worked her clit.

"*Sssshhhiiit*! Yes! You're gonna make me come..."

"I am," I said. "You're so wet, Opal. So hot. You know how hard you make me, knowing this is for me?"

Opal's breaths came in short, ragged gasps as her hips

jerked. I felt her thighs trembling, her body coiling tighter with each pass of my fingers over her sensitive flesh.

"Sterling," she breathed, her grip on me tightening. "I'm gonna come!"

In one fluid motion, I lifted her up and laid her back on the couch, discarding my pants and her shorts before settling between her thighs. I paused for a moment, drinking in the sight of her splayed out, hair fanned out on the cushion, her breasts riding each heaving breath. Then I couldn't wait a second longer.

My mouth descended onto hers in a desperate kiss as I pushed inside her. She was so tight, so hot, so juicy I had to pause to catch my breath. Opal's legs wrapped around my waist, pulling me deeper.

"Yeah," she moaned, bucking her hips up to meet mine. "Oh God, Sterling, yes!"

I started with slow, deep strokes, building up a rhythm that had us both gasping and panting within seconds.

"Harder," she panted. "Fuck me hard!"

I obliged, picking up the pace and driving into her with long, deep strokes as my mouth found hers again. We kissed and moved against each other in a desperate flurry.

Her lips parted from mine and she let out a low, keening whine that built higher and louder as I brushed against that sweet spot inside her. I slipped a hand between us to circle her clit, intensifying the already overwhelming sensation.

We moved together, our bodies meeting each other with every thrust. Our breaths were fast and ragged, our skin slick with sweat as we chased our release together.

"Shit..." she whimpered. "You're gonna make me come again..."

"Take it, baby," I whispered against her ear.

I physically felt her let go. Her mouth dropped open as

her orgasm crashed over her, taking her in waves. With quick pulses, her inner walls clenched and released me in rapid rhythm, drawing me deeper.

"Mmmmm...Opal...baby...*yessssss*..." I began a long, low growl as the sight, the sound, the sensation of her release triggered mine. My hips stuttered against hers as I emptied myself inside her, groaning her name with each pulse.

We lay there tangled together, catching our breath as the aftershocks rippled through us.

I peppered kisses along her neck and collarbone, reveling in the feel of her skin and the way she fit every part of me so right.

"Just in time to catch the real first episode," said Opal. In the background, the credits were rolling, following the first episode of A Different World.

I laughed, nuzzling into her neck. "What do you say we pause this and take round two in the shower?"

* * *

The first hint of dawn found Opal's body tucked up against mine, two fingers massaging her clit in sensuous circles while I gave her slow, languid strokes from behind as if we had all the time in the world.

"Sterling," she whimpered.

"Yeah, baby," I whispered, nipping at her earlobe, then kissing her shoulder. "What can I do for you?"

She reached back, grabbing my hip and pulling me closer. "Just like this. Don't stop."

I obliged, maintaining the steady rhythm of my hips and hand. The room was quiet, save for our breaths and the sounds of our bodies moving together. There was no urgency, no frantic rush to completion. Just a slow build of pleasure, savoring each other.

Opal's breathing quickened, little gasps and whimpers growing into the most erotic moans. Her hips rocked back against mine, fucking me back with increasing urgency.

"Feeling good, huh?" I murmured, pressing kisses along her shoulder.

"Mmm! So *fucking* good...oh my...God! Don't stop..."

"If I could," I whispered into her ear, "I'd do this with you all day."

"Shit...Sterling...you're gonna make me come...."

"Let's go, baby. Let it go."

She sucked in a long, loud breath, then exhaled, "I'm coming, I'm coming, I'm com—" Her words dissolved into a long, low moan she began to tremble. I held her close, snapping my hips against her ass, adding pressure to my fingers on her clit, sending her into a frenzy.

I felt her orgasm hit her hard. Her pussy clamped down on me in a vise grip, pulsing rhythmically. "Unh! Sterling! Yes, yes, yes!" she screamed, shoving her head into the pillow while her hips bucked uncontrollably.

Her climax triggered mine. I plunged deep inside her with an animalistic grunt and rode her orgasm with her.

After, we stayed connected, bodies trembling, sweat drying, breathless panting returning to normal as we came down from our shared high.

Opal rolled over to face me. "I was never a morning sex person before," she murmured, then pressed a kiss to my chest.

I chuckled, pulling an arm around her to bring her right up against me, cupping a breast in one hand. "I'm here to make sweeping changes in your life, Opal."

"If the sweeping changes involve me getting fucked through the mattress on a regular basis, I will take them."

"You said it, not me."

"I sure did," she replied with a laugh.

"So, if I get up now, I can make you a mean frittata. You game?"

"You cook too? I need to listen to my mother more often." She laughed, the sound vibrating through me. "Tempting. But I have to drive all the way home and change. I already have to take my first meeting from home. Pray my neighbors aren't listening to something about murder."

Reluctantly, I loosened my hold, letting her slip from the bed. I admired the view as she moved around the room.

When she was dressed, she perched on the edge of the mattress, leaning down to brush a kiss across my lips. "Thank you for last night. For...the past week, actually. Mostly for being patient with me."

"Always." I reached up to tuck a stray hair into the bun she'd wrestled her hair back into. "I meant what I said, Opal. I'm in this. However slow we need to go."

"Sex three times in the span of three days is not slow... but I'm starting to believe that's a really good thing."

"Four times, baby," I corrected.

With a final press of her lips to mine, she was gone. The place felt colder in her absence.

* * *

The morning crowd at Coffee Theory was just starting to thin when I arrived. The regulars had settled into their usual spots, laptops open at the communal table. Newspaper readers dominated the leather armchairs and young professionals huddled over tablets in the booths.

Joya looked up from wiping down the counters. "Look who decided to grace us with his presence today," she teased. "I was starting to think you'd found another coffee shop."

"Never." I leaned against the counter. "No one else takes coffee as seriously as you do."

"Flattery will get you everywhere."

"That's what I hear," I muttered, then added, "My usual, please."

She started grinding fresh beans. The scent that filled the cafe after she lifted the lid of the grinder was intoxicating. "You must be so ready for your new office. How long now?"

"Couple weeks, they say. We'll see."

"Construction delays?" She bobbed her head sympathetically. "Welcome to Atlanta. Everything takes twice as long as they say it will."

"So I'm learning." I watched her precise movements as she prepared what I knew would be a perfect cup.

"Well, at least you have a reliable coffee spot in the meantime."

My phone vibrated in my hand. I turned it over to check it, noting Opal's text that she was parking. I smiled, scrolling through a series of messages, then told Joya, "Opal is on her way up from the garage."

Her brows rose slightly, but she nodded and started on the second drink.

When Opal walked in wearing wide-leg dark trousers and a coral silk blouse, her hair in a neat bun, I was already waiting with her americano. She accepted it with a smile that made my heart skip. I couldn't resist leaning in to drop a kiss on her plump lips.

Joya's delighted squeal made us both laugh.

"Oh God, I'm sorry," she said, not looking sorry at all. She clasped her hands and beamed. "But you two are just too cute."

"Come on," I told Opal, nodding toward the window seats. "Let's chill for a minute."

We settled into a pair of chairs tucked into the corner of the cafe where we could watch the morning bustle of midtown Atlanta through the windows. Opal crossed her legs, seeming entirely more relaxed and happy than she'd seemed the day before. She clutched her coffee in both hands as she sipped. A stack of papers peeked out from her messenger bag.

"How'd your first meeting go?" I asked.

"Much better than I expected it to go. And my neighbors must have slept in; no true crime podcasts blasting through the walls."

"Sounds like an okay morning, so far." I leaned back, stretching my arm along the back of the chair next to me. Opal seemed to leer at me as I moved. I didn't really mind.

"Well, we kicked the day off with a nice enough start." Smug, she brought her cup to her lips, but her eyes said so much. "Uhm...so what's your day looking like?"

"Meetings," I replied. "Always meetings. I'm giving a presentation to two potential clients, then some contract reviews and I have a strategy meeting with a startup after lunch. That should be interesting. How about you?"

"Also meetings. Back-to-back code reviews." She took another long sip of coffee, averting her eyes to the hustle and flow outside. "The UI team keeps sending updates that break my back-end code. That's really slowing progress down."

"I have no idea what you just said, but you were hot as fuck saying it. You just sit in your office shouting tech-speak at people all day, don't you?"

"Mostly." She paused, then she perked. "Actually, I'm taking off early today. Asia and I need a last-minute shopping trip before a work event on Saturday. I have a dress but I might take her advice and wear something...not black."

I leaned in, lowering my voice. "I wouldn't mind seeing you in something not black."

"You said you liked me in black."

"I like you in anything," I replied, then added with a wink, "Or...nothing."

She laughed. "Mr. Carter, behave yourself. We're in public."

"By the way..." I took a sip of coffee, watching her, dragging the moment out. "You never answered my question."

"What question? When did you ask me something?" Her brow furrowed. "I'm honestly too exhausted to remember much of anything right now."

"Thank you very much," I replied with a satisfied grin.

She kicked my foot under the table, fighting back a smile.

"The formal event you mentioned...is it Circuit2Soul?"

Her eyes widened and her mouth dropped open. "How do you know about Circuit2Soul? You just got to town."

"I have my sources. Actually, Sedrick got an extra pair of tickets and told me to get a tux. He thinks I need to go. Network. Schmooze. Get my name out there."

"He's right. I didn't even think about that, actually," she answered. "Yes, I'll be presenting the Align Platform at Circuit2Soul this Saturday."

"Do you...happen to have a date for it?"

A half hour later, we stood at the divide between two different elevator banks. The lobby was empty, giving us a moment of privacy.

"Will you have time for lunch if you're leaving early today?" I asked, pulling her close for a kiss that lingered.

"Mmmm," she hummed against my lips. "Don't know. Maybe. I'll send you a sign from the window."

"Or... you could just text me," I told her, laughing. "Let me know where you're at around 12:30. I'll grab you something and bring it to you. The days of you working through lunch are coming to an end."

"Oh, really?"

"Really. Sweeping changes."

"Well, then. I...think I'm going to like dating you."

"You better." I kissed her again just as the doors to her elevator opened. She stepped inside, then turned and gave me a playful wink before the doors closed.

Mine arrived a few moments later. I got in and pulled out my phone. With a grin, because I knew the reaction I would get, I thumbed out a text to Sedrick.

> Is that house in Grant Park still available?

> Don't play with me, Sterling. Why you asking?

> I liked the listing. Price is right. Set me up a tour. Might be time to plant some roots.

> It's about damn time! I'll hit you back with details.

I hopped off the elevator and unlocked my office, heading straight to the windows. I caught Opal at her desk, clearly on a call. Her hands were a flurry of motion and her face was animated as she spoke.

Just as I was about to turn away, she sat back in her chair, picked up her coffee cup, and peered out of the window. I waved; she glanced up, caught my eye, and lifted her coffee cup in a little toast.

Yeah. I'm home.

Epilogue

pal

Bass from Kendrick Lamar's "Not Like Us" pulsed through the St. Regis Atlanta's grand ballroom, the perfect soundtrack for the annual Circuit2Soul Tech Coalition Gala.

I stood at the edge of the dance floor, champagne flute in hand, bumping my shoulders and wishing I could crip-walk as Black excellence moved in sync everywhere—tech innovators, venture capitalists, and entrepreneurs mixing and mingling under crystal chandeliers.

The energy was electric, charged with possibility and promise. The future of technology was being shaped one power move at a time.

I smoothed my hands over the butter-yellow satin of my gown, still hardly believing Asia talked me into such a bold choice. The draping emphasized my curves while maintaining sophistication, and the color made my deep brown skin glow. The coordinating scarf ramped up the elegance.

When I emerged from Sterling's guest bedroom after getting ready, he stopped mid-stride in the living room, his eyes traveling the length of me with such naked appreciation. I couldn't help but preen a little under his attention.

"It's not black," I said, gushing. "Isn't it pretty?"

"*Daaaaamnnnn*," he swooned, then gave a soft cough. "I mean... you look absolutely stunning, Opal."

I'd taken my own moment to appreciate him in his tuxedo, paying special attention to the bow tie I watched him tie in the mirror. It felt intimate, domestic even, getting ready together in his space, the kind of moment that made me think maybe Asia had been right about more than just the dress.

Now, an hour after my presentation, I could finally breathe. The Align platform demo exceeded my expectations. The interface was sleek and intuitive, the analytics compelling, and most importantly, the mission had resonated. I'd watched faces in the crowd light up with understanding as I'd explained how the platform could transform hiring practices and workplace culture.

The questions afterward were thoughtful and engaged. No one tried to mansplain diversity initiatives to me or suggest that merit alone should determine hiring. Instead, CEOs and HR executives clustered around my demo station to learn more about implementation timelines and customization options.

There was a minuscule flaw that no one noticed but me —I filed it away to deal with first thing Monday morning. Right now it was time to celebrate.

"And here I was thinking I'd be the one turning heads tonight." Asia's voice carried over the music as she and

Jordan approached, her backless, sparkling silver gown catching the light with every movement. Her locs were pulled into a regal high ponytail and accented with a silver scarf. My best friend could never be subtle.

"You are turning heads," said Jordan. "I've counted at least three people almost walking into walls."

I turned to embrace her, careful not to spill our champagne.

"And you," Asia pulled back to admire my dress again, "finally listened about wearing color. You are an absolute vision in yellow. I might cry."

"You wore me down," I admitted. "Especially when you begged me to not look like a funeral director at this gala."

"It worked, didn't it?" Asia gestured at my dress triumphantly. "When's the last time anyone saw Opal Richardson at a formal event not dressed like she's auditioning for Morticia Addams?"

"I wear other colors," I protested weakly.

"Navy blue and charcoal don't count as colors," they chorused in unison, then broke into laughter.

"There he is!" A booming voice cut through the crowd. "Lil bro! No more holding out!"

I turned to see a broadly built man in a tuxedo approaching with a stunning woman in a red gown on his arm. Sterling's brother Sedrick—had to be, given the family resemblance in their smiles, was already reaching to pull Sterling into a back-slapping hug.

"This must be the famous Opal," Sedrick said, turning to me with his arms open wide and a grin that was pure mischief.

"Sedrick," Sterling warned, but I could hear the affection in his voice.

"Don't mind him," the woman said, extending her hand

when he finally released me. "My husband is just excited because he's been trying to get Sterling back to Atlanta for years. The Align demo was incredible," she added. "Everyone's talking about it."

"Opal, let us know when you're ready to double date. I'm piling up all the stories I can think of to embarrass Sterling. You need to hear them all. And there are some baby pictures—"

"Okay!" Sterling cut in quickly. "Don't you have some networking to do? Somebody across the room wants to buy a house. I'm sure of it."

"I'm just getting started." Sedrick turned back to me. "Has he told you about his brief stint in an R&B group in college?"

"Somehow that tidbit did not come out in our game of Two Truths and a Lie." I couldn't help but laugh at Sterling's pained expression. "I'd love to hear all about it."

"Woman after my own heart," Sedrick declared. "Blair, we're keeping her."

"We sure are," Blair agreed, looping her arm through mine. "Come on, Opal. Let me tell you about the time these two tried to start a lawn care business and ended up setting the neighbor's rose bush on fire."

"That was all Sedrick," Sterling called after us, but I was already being led away, giggling with Blair.

By the time Sterling rescued me fifteen minutes later, I had heard enough embarrassing stories about the Carter brothers to last months. More importantly, I had a sense of the close dynamic between brothers and the strong family bonds that had shaped the man I was falling for.

"Look at you, holding court." Sterling's voice was honey in my ear as his hand settled at the small of my back. He pressed a fresh glass of champagne into my free hand.

"Have I mentioned how proud I am of you? You did your thing, baby."

I turned to face him, unable to suppress my smile. He was devastating in his tuxedo, the perfect fit emphasizing his broad shoulders and trim waist. The crisp white of his shirt made his skin luminous, and his signature diamond stud winked in his ear.

"Only a few times in the last hour," I teased. "I'd like to hear it a few more times later tonight."

"Bet." He clinked our glasses together. "I don't think I've ever seen anything sexier than you explaining how your algorithm identifies bias in job descriptions. Just..." He growled. "Lights me right up."

I laughed, a real belly laugh that had several heads turning our way. "You *would* find coding sexy."

"No, baby. I find *you* sexy." His thumb traced circles on my back through the silk. "Though I won't lie, watching you own that room in this dress didn't hurt."

If I could, I'd drag him into one of the hotel's luxury suites and show him exactly how much I appreciated his support. Instead, I forced myself to maintain composure.

"So...in this R&B group you were in...did y'all dance?"

"Only the hottest moves. Still got 'em."

"Prove it," I challenged, taking his hand and leading him to the dance floor. The DJ had switched to "Outstanding" by The Gap Band. I turned in his arms, swaying to the music and fighting the urge to start a soul train line.

"You look like you're analyzing something," Sterling murmured against my hair. "What are you thinking about?"

"How good this feels," I admitted. "This moment right here. Right now. I feel good. And I love it. It just feels right."

"That's because it is right." His arms tightened around me. "Everything is perfectly... *aligned.*"

I groaned, lifting my head to glare at him. "Did you really just make a platform pun?"

His laugh rumbled through his chest. "Couldn't resist. But I mean it." His expression grew serious. "I'm all in, Opal. Whatever comes next, I'm here for all of it."

"Uhm...funny you should mention what comes next..." I smirked, spotting two familiar figures approaching through the crowd. "I hope you're ready to meet Doctors Richardson, because they're about ten feet behind you and closing in fast."

Sterling's composure never wavered as he turned. My parents approached, both elegant in formal wear—my father in a tailored tuxedo, my mother resplendent in a black gown. They wore identical expressions of keen interest that would have made me nervous if I wasn't standing next to Sterling.

I stepped forward to embrace them both, then turned back to Sterling, reaching for his hand. "I'd like you to meet my boyfriend, Sterling Carter."

"Dr. Richardson," Sterling said, shaking my father's hand firmly. "And Dr. Richardson." He turned to my mother with a wide smile. "Opal speaks so highly of you both. I understand you're responsible for the brilliant mind I've been admiring since I met her."

My mother's eyebrow rose, but I caught the slight upturn of her lips. "We merely provided the foundation. Opal has always charted her own course."

"Yes she has," my father agreed, his eyes twinkling. "Though I noticed you had quite a few questions during her presentation. You seemed very engaged for someone in public relations."

"I want to understand the work thoroughly," Sterling replied smoothly. "And I had the feeling some had questions and didn't want to ask them. Besides, who wouldn't be fascinated by someone revolutionizing the way companies approach inclusion?"

"Indeed." My father's expression brightened. "Perhaps you'd like to join us for Sunday dinner next weekend? We could discuss your perspective on the tech scene in more detail."

I squeezed Sterling's hand—not because I was scared, or as a warning. It was a squeeze of joy. My father may as well have stamped his approval across Sterling's forehead.

I wasn't afraid of what came next. I was ready for it, all of it, with this man who'd stormed past my every defense.

I lifted my face for a kiss, not caring who saw. We had aligned... and I was never letting go.

Thank you so much for supporting my work! If you loved this novella, please spread the good word! Please don't forget to review this title on your social media, at Goodreads or Storygraph.

Also, if you're not on my newsletter, you didn't get the heads up when this book dropped. **FIX THAT HERE and get a free short story, Olympia's on King Street.**

Have you met Kwame and Thandie? Snatch up my most recent release, **The Festival at Evergreen Falls,** available in eBook.

Books by DL White

Find Books and Merch at Booksbydlwhite.com/shop

Brunch at Ruby's, a Ruby's novel

Dinner at Sam's, a Ruby's novel

Beach Thing, a Black Diamond Romance

Elysium, a Black Diamond Vacation Romance

The Pearl at Black Diamond, a Black Diamond Romance

Leslie's Curl & Dye, a Potter Lake Small Town Romance

Second Time Around, a Potter Lake Holiday Short

The Guy Next Door, a Potter Lake Small Town Romance

Home for the Holidays, A Potter Lake Holiday Novella

The Kwanzaa Brunch, a Holiday Short

A Thin Line

The Never List

Hey, Lover, a Second Chance Romance

Unexpected, a holiday short

The Festival at Evergreen Falls

Calculated Risk (*Coming Spring 2025*)